Pull Gently, Tear Here

Pull Gently, Tear Here

stories by
Alexandra Leggat

INSOMNIAC PRESS

Edited by Mike O'Connor
Copy edited by Christine Schuler
Designed by Mike O'Connor

Canadian Cataloguing in Publication Data

Leggat, Alexandra, 1964-
    Pull gently, tear here: stories

ISBN 1-895837-75-8

I. Title.

PS8573.E461716P84 2000   C813'.54   C00-932-233-7
PR9199.3.L44P84 2000

The publisher gratefully acknowledges the support of the Canada Council, the Ontario Arts Council and Department of Canadian Heritage through the Book Publishing Industry Development Program.

Printed and bound in Canada

Insomniac Press, 192 Spadina Avenue, Suite 403,
Toronto, Ontario, Canada, M5T 2C2
www.insomniacpress.com

THE CANADA COUNCIL | LE CONSEIL DES ARTS
FOR THE ARTS | DU CANADA
SINCE 1957 | DEPUIS 1957

ONTARIO ARTS
COUNCIL
CONSEIL DES ARTS
DE L'ONTARIO

For my Mum & Dad, always

Table of Contents

I'm gonna start a revolution from my bed
'Cause you said the brains I had went to my head...

"Don't Look Back in Anger," Oasis

So You Think

The day lies like a newborn foal at your feet. All long-legged and clumsy, eyes barely open and sleepy looking. It grapples to its feet. It makes you smile and want to help it find its balance, but you know it's got to learn to stand on its own. You lie back on your pillows and let your eyes close, letting yourself fall back into sleep. Now you've seen the most exciting part of the day.

Only the sound of the kettle could entice you up and out of bed and if there were someone there to make tea, you'd let them make it and bring it to you. It's not that you're lazy, just tired. And each day is not without some kind of agenda; and time is something that only runs out. Your body's heavy. Mind spinning like a twister. Uprooting all things and sending them hurling across your view, crashing down in parts of you that can't stand the reminder.

London School

I remember being thrown in the nettles in Form 1 by one of the big girls. Her ponytail swayed across her back like a thoroughbred's as she trotted away. It was longer than I was tall. I can remember the pounding of my heart in my head, walking down the hall, and it didn't help knowing my mother was teaching upstairs. And there was a boy in her class whose teeth were chillingly yellow and decrepit. His family couldn't afford the dentist and all he ate at school were Licorice Allsorts and toffee. I would never want to make him laugh or have him fancy me for fear he'd smile and I'd shiver so blatantly he'd be hurt.

The bread pudding towered out of the china bowl at lunchtime and those were the days you had to eat everything in front of you. These days, it would be considered a form of abuse. The mince and the too-mashed tatties I could stomach. Even the liver. But I'd lose sleep over the bread pudding.

Swimming classes; twelve children made to swim in a too

small above-ground pool, the water about as warm as the rain that was almost always spewing from the English sky.

I'd bury myself in my towel before and after and think, if I could see the shade of blue my lips must be, it might be a shade I'd like.

I wonder why I never spoke up, never spoke about the girls throwing me in the nettles. Spoke up about the food I didn't like, and the cold water, and the boy with the yellow teeth. You just did things even if you didn't want to. Too afraid to say no. To say no, was not the done thing. I'd say a lot to myself loudly, often deafeningly. It was there I learned, don't speak until spoken to. Don't speak.

The Innocence and
the Ingenuity of the Fool

There was the summer you rode the carousel around and around and around. You'd get off and get back in line and give the man your tickets and get back on. We were twenty. You said it didn't matter so much that it wouldn't get you anywhere—but at least you were moving.

I remember keeping my head down and looking away when you waved. I remember getting hot with embarrassment and anger and boredom. And I wondered why the carousel operator let you ride it at your age and why he let you ride it for hours. You always took the nicest horse. The white one that held its head and tail most confidently. And I knew that if it were real it would have a nice temperament and an even gate. Strong but nice.

You came down from the ride smiling. How you were not dizzy and disoriented amazed me. And you could eat Pogos and beer-nuts while everything in and around me was spinning from watching you. You would go back the next day and it sickened me. And there was no way of getting around your carnival philosophies. So I told you I'd never accompany you there again and you sulked the whole way home.

I took the teddybear I won smashing Coke bottles with a baseball and shoved it in the trash. It's the only thing I'd won skillfully. I told you I was through with adolescence and I meant it.

You sat on the curb and put your head low. You muttered something about not knowing what to do now that I was growing up without you. I told you there are people you can talk to about that kind of thing and you laughed.

I looked out at the suburban landscape where we'd kicked cans, rode bikes across, went to birthday parties and bush parties and ran track and field on.

I watched the neighbour's bedroom lights go out, one by one, and wondered, if I stayed here would my lights be out by ten when I reached forty.

You touched your knee to my knee and said nothing. I heard your dog barking. He could tell we were at the foot of the driveway. He'd been listening to our foot-of-the-driveway conversations for years. You said you'd call me tomorrow, got up and walked inside.

I caught the last bus to my brother's house on the other side of town. I knew he'd be up and lonely, and probably have beer. We talked about predictable childhoods and carousel rides. He told me I was too old for the suburbs but too young for the city. I drank my beer faster to drown out his sense of logic. I stared out the window at the empty road, at the dying bulb in the nearest street light. I wondered if maybe the next day I should mount that wooden horse and let it take me around and around—just to see where it takes you.

Boomerang

I look up into the sky and wonder where all the birds have gone. The woman that looks after this house calls out for me like I've been missing for hours, not minutes.

Inside, my mother's aroma lingers in the kitchen. There's no mistaking her presence here, between the woman that looks after this house and the kitchen sink. Telling stories about how she'd shocked someone at work again. You'd never guess she had the devil in her. Dear Ma.

I wonder if the woman who looks after this house is ever lonely babysitting a too-empty family home. My big brother's in the South eleven months out of twelve. My sister's busy up-town with two children and a husband that loves her. Mother's fancy-footed, skipping across the world in a defiant wonderment and Dad's strapped to her luggage—trying desperately to catch his breath. I'm at the summer cottage with my head buried in books and empty pages waiting for a great thought. I barely come out in the light, but to venture back to my childhood home and see if the woman who looks after this house is still living, and if I might happen upon a member of my family to comfort me and remind me of what it's like not to be alone.

The woman who looks after this house is old enough to be dead now. Although she looks more alive than me. She's cared for this house since before mother and dad lived here. Before any of us kids lived. Since her mother looked after this house for some nineteenth-century poet. Apparently her mother wasn't very interested in literature and was none the wiser about whom she was working for. So it's been debated as to who it was. Some say Byron, some say Blake. I wish it was Keats but it was probably no one anyone but his own mother knew. Dad says it must have been someone brilliant. He always says the nicest things.

My big sister is naturally oblivious and unambitious. She was scouting for a husband before she could walk—was probably hoping to find one so she wouldn't have to learn how to. She would have let all of us live her life for her. To mother, of course, this was ideal. Open your mouth daughter, I've some words to put in it.

My sister is satisfied with her beauty alone. It's her biggest accomplishment to date. I suppose I don't blame her. If I were that lovely on the outside, I think I would more than likely be satisfied as well. She has a wealthy, handsome husband who dotes on her and actually looks like he really does love her. He holds her hand and squeezes her shoulder when he walks by her at family gatherings.

The children are picture-perfect and spoiled rotten. The little girl wears fancy dresses and takes violin lessons. The boy is cocky and tall and acts like he was born with a Ph.D.

The woman who looks after this house puts a pot of tea on the table for the hundredth millionth time in her life. I've tried to serve her but she won't have it. Some things you're just born to do—I think—and I don't understand why more of us don't fight that. After tea, I wander up into dad's library and poke around amongst the too-old books. I never thought I'd reach a stage where I felt that some authors are simply too dead to read; but tonight I just want to stare at their spines. It's quiet here, even for me. I can hear the dust fall. From somewhere, I can—I think—hear a sound like my mother crying, streaming through the halls. I knew she cried. I would have been there for her. I still could—if she'd let me.

I go slowly to her room. It's crisp and immaculate. Nothing's touched, like no one ever really lived in here. Her pillows remain puffy and huge like autumn clouds; as inflated as the day they were bought, probably over twelve years ago. Her books neatly piled on the bedside table. The classics. Only the best for mother.

I sit down on the edge of her bed. Close my eyes and let my life drift back to where it came from.

A Watched Pot

His hand came off my knee. His eyes glazed over, like if he didn't focus on me, I'd disappear. And consequently, I tried. Couldn't lose myself in the crowded bar. No vacant corners to hide in. No secret walls to escape through. I moved up and over slowly towards the door. Didn't turn around to see him waving. He wouldn't be waving—I know—couldn't face the truth, didn't want to see the lack of goodbye tidings. Just wanted to kid myself into believing he was genuinely sorry to see me leave—was at least watching me leave.

The other girl who lives in this house descends the stairs slowly—knowingly. Sees me sitting with my knees in my arms, head resting on them, looking low. Says to me, you're not sitting there waiting for the phone to ring are you? I say no, I'm sitting here waiting for the day to end. Tomorrow he'll be one day longer gone. She knows it's not worth crying over.

I try to take the knots out of my stomach. Feel a sense of resignation when he drops by on the hottest afternoon we've had so far this summer, and asks me how I am.

Said he needs to talk and is it true I'm really seeing Buddy now 'cause he knows him and isn't too fond of him. Doesn't understand the union. I sprouted roots elsewhere and he sat around in smoky pubs watering himself to no avail.

He left and I watched him cross the road with his shoulders hunched and a sorry gait like a wounded horse.

He calls unexpectedly with excitement in his voice. Says he called me last night at four in the morning but only let it ring twice on account of the time. There was a day I could have caught the phone on one ring. When the phone rings you wish it was the guy and when it's your best friend or your mother or anyone other than him you sink and wish you'd never answered it. Now at least I know I can sleep through that ring and just be pleased by the fact he'd attempted to call.

I tell him I was worried about him. He said he was sorry and talked like I mattered in his future. I said he's got to let me know where I stand. He strayed off in another direction. I let it go. Hoping we'd run back into it. He spoke with a tone a little more than like and I thought he was going to tell me something I wanted to hear. I could practically feel it coming to the surface.

He said goodbye without a thread left holding us till the next time. I reached into my shoebox, the one that keeps pieces of paper with people's phone numbers on them that I've been too lazy to put into my book. I call Buddy. He's not there.

The other girl who lives in this house walks through the front door. Sees me sitting in the chair with the phone in my hands. Says, you're not sitting there waiting for the phone to ring are you? I say no, I'm waiting for the kettle to boil.

Just the Ghost in You

You stood at the mouth of the laneway that led to the old, white house you were brought up to fear. For years you rode by it, fast. Felt a haunting breeze blow up from the woods that enveloped it. Thought you heard a shrill scream, a low ache escaping its rooms. Swore you saw lights through the trees when nobody had lived there in years. You thought it was eerie. You knew it was sad.

When you were sixteen, you dated a boy who drove a cool, black Firebird. He was the love of your life up till then. You'd heard rumours he'd take girls down to the white house and make out with them in the driveway. Sometimes he'd make them get out and sit on the front porch. Every girl broke up with him those nights. Guess those were the girls he didn't really want to go out with, just wanted to kiss them and scare them and leave them leaving him. He never took you there. He never drove you on empty streets. He did leave you standing on the corner of a busy downtown street once. He didn't take you there. He never arrived.

When you came back home after years of being elsewhere, you rode your old bike to the lake. You thought about old friends and boyfriends and the music you'd listened to and the dreams you had. You saw the naked silhouettes of your pals and you splashing in and out of the water like clumsy adolescent dolphins. You laughed with the memory of the laughter, and the shrieks and the pranks you played on each other. You laughed and it rippled the calm in you.

The ride back to your old house was chilly. The sun set early and you wondered if it had something to do with you. You stopped for a rest by the white house. You caught a breath and it was taken away before you had time to feel the good of it. You thought you saw lights flickering through the trees, shadows passing by the windows. You thought you heard it call your name and you rode like a racehorse home. You fell onto your knees on the front yard of your old house and you panted till the dog came, licking life back into you.

One morning you woke determined. Rode down the laneway to the white house. Even the dog's hair was standing on its back. You both approached nervously and felt hearts pressing through bones to escape. You felt the house huge in front of you, then you felt it cave in when it saw you. You'd caught it on a bad day, all its defenses weakened by time. All its ghosts vacated. All yours just arrived.

Visions of Jack

Y ou sit there in your gray flannel suit. You with that I've-been-to-all-knowing-and-back-twice look. You with your umpteen novels and bad-alcohol-poisoning death certificate. I can sympathize. Your picture on my wall and all your words ingested in my little head, and I can't touch you like you touch me. Can't bring you back, pour you red wine and listen to jazz in my apartment in the suburbs. Can't. All the dream boys are dead and I'm not supposed to cry about it anymore. I'm not supposed to grieve.

I hear the shuffle of a ghost's footsteps coming down my hall. I feel the warmth of the past and it's just the apparition I've been waiting for. I've been waiting for you.

And he walks into my room, taller than his pictures, thinner and of course paler. This is his ghostly side. I want to hide beneath my covers, tremble and cry. But I'd regret not embracing this haunting and take him into my arms, if ghosts don't float through arms; and say, you are who I dream of—dead or alive.

And he will be happy. I will make sure of that.

He stays till the distant dawn threatens to light up the place. He leaves slowly like it's tough to go. I know he'll be back. But he's not sure. He can't leave me anything. Nothing to prove he was here.

I've got the picture of his gray-flannel-suit-self on my wall. I've got his umpteen novels on my shelf and his ghostly scent in my bed.

Dodger

You wander down an alley lined with flaming oil drums. Passed a group of dirty, drunken men trying to keep warm. They lift paper bags shaped like bottles up to their cracking lips. You listen to them converse in grunts and cackles and think you wandered into the beginning of time when men were apes and women weren't invented yet. They don't notice you. You can't entice them with a taste of things to come. You move on like women do.

You imagine the life of the men in the alley. A sad home with a mother who cared too much for the wrong man and that man drank too much, and brought his hand across the boy's face one too many times and told him he was stupid and pathetic and had his mother's feeble eyes. And she stays in the corner shaking her head afraid to move, afraid to stand up for her own boy for fear of that man's fists on her instead of him.

He runs away at sixteen, say, goes to the alley and is given a warm handshake and a swig of something that burns as it oozes down his throat, but leaves him feeling warm. He steals from corner stores and suit pockets, little girls and old ladies. He shares his wealth with the pack he hangs out with. They pat his back and tell him he's a good boy.

He falls in love one day, say, with the girl who starts working for her dad at the hardware store. He spots her through the window as he's passing by. She laughs silently with some woman. He can't hear her through the glass. He can only watch her motions, her eyes sparkling like birthday candles, her hair swaying slightly down her shapely back. Her hands clutching onto each other for comfort. She's shy. He senses that. He touches the glass with both his hands, runs them down the length of her. She doesn't feel a thing.

He takes back a smile and a sparkle in his eyes to his cardboard shack. He takes a swig of the burning tonic and dreams with his eyes wide open about the hardware girl. Him in a suit and tie and her in diamonds and nothing more. He brings her flowers and she makes him warm dinners. She holds him and tells him she loves him and they kiss and he sits up shaking his head, puts his head in his hands, punches the ground with his fists.

You move past a woman begging for change in front of a corner store. She's got a sign hanging round her neck. You think you read something like help please my child and something about a dog and other things under a roof she can't afford.

At least she has a roof, you think and wonder what happens if she dies, to the child and cats and dogs. And you wonder why it is these people have children, cats and dogs, as you wander by childless with money in your pocket.

You breeze by and the sign sways. She brushes the hair out of her eyes and looks around. You stop and turn. You stand above her and drop bills into her hat.

She watches astonished at the magic money falling from nowhere.

A young boy appears out of the corner of your eye. You turn to watch him reach into his pocket and go into the corner store. You follow him in. You see him turn around and see you. You scream. He grabs cash and whatever's close on the shelves, cigarettes and things. You hear the owner's heart pounding through the scuffles, you look up to see his tears and he sees your tears and you watch each other helplessly as the young boy flees. The beggar woman's packed it in for the day.

You rise in pieces. A moment in slow motion, then everything moves too fast: the men in blue with caps on their heads and guns attached to the hip, the red river flowing through the soda pop and chips aisle, the men in orange pressing down hard on the trembling store-owner's chest, and the arms reaching towards you, motioning you to the door.

Lips moving, eyes staring into the core of you. No sound. No sense. Just bits and pieces of some nightmare you woke up in.

They lead you to a car with a caged-back seat, put you in it and slam the door. You sit. You just sit and look at your knees. Look at you hands. Release your fists, see your fingernails have tattooed little smiles into your palms. You look out the window at the commotion. All the bystanders shaking heads, and shrugging shoulders; hands over mouths, tears running from every other one's eyes. The car pulls away from the scene. You wonder where you're going, what you've done. You put your thumping head in your hands. You cry dry tears. You watch heads turn as the car moves by. Scrutinizing eyes looking in at you. You feel small—criminal. The car stops at a light. You focus in on four boys sitting on the steps of a fallen down brownstone. They're laughing and smoking cigarettes. You're drawn to the quieter one. The one smirking and gazing off into the distance. The one the others are cajoling. He shrugs them off and puffs on his cigarette. The car moves on. You turn and watch him through the back window, neck strained, till he disappears.

They tell you they're taking you to the station to ask you a few questions. You think about exactly what happened. The faces, the face. Can you recall what they looked like, how old, how tall, what colour? You look out the back window, put a finger to your lips and whisper...SSSH!

They lead you down a gray hall, into a cold room: one window, one table, one light, two chairs. Just like television. They leave you alone. You wonder where the ashtray is.

A man will come in with dishevelled hair, an open collar shirt, probably pale blue and gray dress pants. He'll have a coffee in a styrofoam cup and a cigarette dangling from his mouth. He'll talk loudly and treat you like you've committed the crime. Your only crime was being in the wrong place at the wrong time. Or was it? You wait and you wait. Your head splitting. Your mouth dry like flour. Your stomach empty. Someone comes in behind you. You're beyond caring.

She touches your shoulder. Asks if you're okay. You tell her you're thirsty and she motions to someone behind you, and you hear the door close. She tells you her name is constable something, that a man has been murdered and the murderer is out there on the streets now as she speaks, and it's up to you to give them all the information they need to catch the monster. You blink twice. Feel yourself getting dizzy. You watch the one light spinning in the air above you. You watch the constable clone herself in front of you. She's doubled then tripled. You feel hot and sick and then you fall onto the table in front of you. You wake up in a white room. You tell them you can't remember a thing. They send you home with a telephone number and a *please, please rack your brain, Miss.* You agree to call if you think of anything. You drop the number in a garbage bin.

Days go by and you can't leave the house. Can't take your hand off your heart or keep your eyes dry. You wonder who you're weeping for. A man killed on his convenience store floor. The woman who can't feed her cats and dogs and child. The boy who dreams of hardware girls and a hot meal. Or yourself.

You can't forget the boy, his hungry eyes. You justify to yourself that you didn't see him shoot the gun, it could have been someone else. He could have been set up. You lie sleepless and wonder if he'll do it again. If you should march right down to the station and describe the boy to them? Right down to the scar on his left hand. The deep line you noticed as he raised his hand to hit the man. You closed your eyes before his hand connected to skin. You shake your head loose of the memories and wonder if he'll ever grow up to be something worthwhile.

The weather felt cooler than usual when you packaged up your conscience and ventured out. You shivered and sighed and watched your breath fog the path in front of you. You wore black so as not to be noticed. You were being noticed. The oil drums alight and surrounded like before. You couldn't see the boy. You marched through the suspicious stares to the street and looked around. Looked up and down at the stillness. Watched a black cat cross the street fast. Saw lights go off. No cars. No other forms of life. Just you and the long gone cat.

Second Skin

Second part

He flashes by the girl of his dreams. She's in the blue dress—the baby blue dress. The one she was wearing when he first laid eyes on her. She's older now. Doesn't look as good in baby blue. She's smiling and she's got a look on her face like she's waiting for someone and he knows it's not him. It was never him and that's what hurts. She's waiting for someone he'll never be and he stopped trying to change himself a long time ago. Didn't have the conviction. Didn't have the cash. He used to watch her. Watch her for hours. Watch her laughing with her friends. Watch her full, red lips moving and smiling and saying all sorts of things to her wide-eyed girlfriends. He used to pretend they were talking about him. He wanted more than anything to know what they were saying. To have some idea how she spoke. He passes by her for the last time.

Sitting in his father's Cadillac waiting for the light to change. He's gripping the wheel like a race-car driver—white knuckled.

He's licking his drying lips and gazing, blankly through the windshield. There's no one next to him. He's going to race himself. Burst through the green light with the gas peddle shoved to the floor. He's going to get to the next light first. He's full-on speeding down the main street of his small hometown. The empty street. The abandoned street. He's racing against time and he's racing to leave all the memories he's accumulated since birth. Hopes they're going to fly out of him when he whips the car around the next turn. He's going as fast as he can to escape the past and he might just do it this time. He might just make it through the finish line a new man—a man.

He sees another woman. A new woman. One he's never met. He slows the car down. He pulls over and stops. She moves through the fog with her head down and her shoes in her hand. Her hair, long and straggly, falling down her back in clumps. She's in a thin dress that's gripping her body like a second skin. He watches her reach into her little bag and pull out a cigarette. She stops at a bench, drops herself onto it and lights the cigarette. Takes a drag and leans back against the bench—relieved. She closes her eyes and smokes. He can't take his eyes off of her. Wonders if she's real. Wonders why she's not worried, how she can sit on a bench at dawn, in the middle of town in a tight thin dress, barefooted and alone, smoking with ease like she was in her own backyard.

He feels his heart warm at the thought of her arms wrapped around him. He bets she has a husky voice and although she's wandering around town at dawn with no shoes on, he bets she has a good head on her shoulders. And when she brushes her hair, she must look beautiful, even more beautiful than she does now. She finishes her cigarette and throws it onto the road. He turns off the radio. Watches her in silence. Wants to get out of the car and introduce himself but he doesn't want to scare her.

He wants to somehow get out of the car without her seeing and stroll by like he walked that way every morning and she just happened to be there in his path this morning. And he can make some point about it, then they'd start talking. Then maybe he'd find out where she's been, where she came from.

She reaches into the bag again and pulls out two things. One she flips open and looks in, straightens her eyebrows and powders her face. Tries to smooth down her hair a bit. The other she applies to her lips, full-on red. As red as the traffic lights he's been dodging all night—as red, redder, than his blood. She puts on her shoes. Stands up and straightens her dress. Pulls it down and over a little. She lights up another cigarette and looks around. He starts the car, attracting her attention. She sees the idle car now and smiles. He tenses his muscles, wonders what she's thinking. Wonders if she'll let him drive her home, if she's thinking he's here to save her. Just happened to appear here now when she was wondering how the hell she was going to get home. Maybe she's not even from around here. He's never seen a woman like that in this town. None so beautiful, so fearless.

The heels of her shoes echo through the emptiness of the barren town as she struts across the road to the car. He rolls down his window with a nice smile. A can-I-help-you-ma'am smile—non-threatening. She's so close. He's so nervous, like when a dream's coming true. She stops at his door, leans down so that her face is inches from his. He looks away. Looks at the time. She says hi, in a whisper. He reaches into his pocket grabs a handful of bills, throws them at her and drives away. Leaving behind all the loving he just invested in.

Postpartum

I show up with Mexico City poems and a bad thought oozing from my eyes. He looks up and back down without a word. Disappointment isn't shocking anymore. I am not predictable by nature, it's simply something I've acquired. He gets up and dresses and tells me this place isn't big enough for us. It's a place he feels crowded in when me and all my demons come home at the end of a day. I tell him I'm planning to renovate.

He leaves and I realize I didn't get to read him the poems. He would have liked the poems and I bought a particular bottle of wine and new candles, and as he walks out the door I wonder what it is I want exactly. I want to tell him I like having him around from time to time but prefer waking up alone in the morning. I don't mind falling asleep with him, I just don't want him here when I open my eyes.

The next morning he calls and he calls. I'm trying to sleep. I know it's him because he's the only one who insists on calling before noon. I have no idea what I'm going to say when I wake and have to return all those calls. I have to somehow answer those ailing messages with the right prescription of words to make him feel better. A prescription I'm not qualified to write. I keep on hoping he'll just fall in love with someone else and I'll be off the hook. I'll miss him for awhile then slowly relax.

There's a knock at the door. I drag myself to it just as the phone rings. I sign for a box of something obviously floral that's almost as long as me, then run for the phone.

"Did you get my flowers? I've been calling to see if you got the flowers," he says.

"You've been calling before the flowers had even bloomed."

"You haven't received them?"

"I haven't opened them. Should I expect something different than yesterday?"

He sends me flowers and more flowers: bouquets, bunches, gardens of flowers, day after day after day. The living room is overflowing. Like I died and this is my funeral. I walk past the room and feel dead. They're not exuding love. They're exuding sympathy. Sorry you passed away. Sorry you're crazy. Sorry you can't make up your mind. Sorry you're afraid to fall in love—to be loved. Damn flowers.

I unplug the phone and attempt to go back to sleep, dream of drifting away somewhere, anywhere without phones, without vegetation. Start again anonymous. Only look at boys but don't touch or talk to them because it causes too many problems. I remember telling him, I was thinking of joining a convent. He said they wouldn't have me. I told him my biggest sin was him.

The phone has fifteen messages, I didn't think that was possible. They're all from the botanist. I hang up the phone and attempt to strangle it with its cord. He turns blue in my mind. See him hunched over himself, head shaking. See him smoking and staring into the distance, saying things to himself like, what have I done, what more can I do and I can't take this anymore. I just can't take this anymore—but he does.

There's a knock at the door. Please, no more flowers. It's him, with a look in his eyes like madness. He's pale and shaky. Beads of sweat forming on his brow, above his lip.

He says, "You're not answering your phone."

"I'm not watering my flowers either. Shall I call the police?"

"Because you're not answering your phone?"

"Because you look like you're going to kill me," I say.

He says, "I just want to talk to you."

I agree to meet him for a coffee elsewhere. I want to go and I don't want to go. I want us to be relative strangers again. I want to go back to the beginning when I was intrigued by him, not scared of him like now.

I look down to avoid his eyes. I tell him he's swell but I want to be alone. I see that he's hurt. I want to disappear under the table, slither across the floor and out the door. I want him to forget he ever laid eyes on me, that he ever laid me.

Dairy Product

We drink to our friendship. To what we think is special at two a.m. as we endure each other's stories of the continual plight for men. Over another drink and another drink, we ponder and droop, ponder and droop—as the drunken do. She tells me her boyfriend's creamy. Sweet. Smooth. Soft. I tell her my boyfriend's like a wave, he can't be immobile, has to keep moving and I'm stuck on him by the bittersweet glue of dreams.

I take a taxi driven by the old man that knows more about my comings and goings than my own old man. She waits for her cream-boy and a concern or two about his expiration date—even she knows some things are too good to last.

I wake the next morning holding my pounding head. Cursing myself for spending too much money, drinking and smoking. I let the dog out, go back to bed and can't sleep because I feel too ill. The dog knows I'm ailing. He won't be walked till mid-afternoon and I won't be playful. I'll be quiet, introspective. I'll gaze out into space, occasionally looking around to see where he is—the dog.

The other wakes unaffected. A big smile on her face. Satisfied and not denied. She'll drift through another day. She'll leave sweet notes for him. He'll call.

She'll grin from ear to ear. And do it all again when the sun goes down, when the last drink goes down, when he lays her down.

I sit across from the one with floppy brown hair. The one that makes me laugh and think, I made a mistake when it came to not falling into his arms when they were held open for me. The one I can sit across from now and know I've got a good friend—at least. I tell him of my Havana dreams, my plans of moving to Spain, of flying to Japan all on a pauper's penny and high hopes. He tells me I have an idea a minute. I laugh. Laugh and shake my head at myself, at my dollar-a-day-dreams, at my sins. All caught up in what could be, and the things that are, just don't phase me anymore.

He tells me he's happy. He can't imagine not going to sleep in his new love's arms. Can't imagine his apartment without her girl things, her perfume, her silhouette walking through the door when he's half-asleep. I tell him I'm happy for him and mostly I am. I am for him and for her, and my friend and her cream-boy and all the others that go to sleep with someone to call their own. I go to sleep with my dog and him with his bone. We've all got something to get us through the night.

Sleeping Dogs Lie

The paper boy throws the paper from the bottom of the lane and hits the window. It doesn't break but it makes some kind of noise and awakens the sleeping one, abruptly, from his fully-clothed sleep on the uncomfortable chair in the living room. He sleeps the whole night like that. Not even woken up by his discomfort, kept asleep by his drunkenness. She walks in and shakes her head. Gave up trying to wake him a long time ago. Learnt to let sleeping dogs lie.

She grabs the paper and goes back to bed. She hears him stretch and yell out something about coffee. She fills in another word in the crossword. Knows he'll be annoyed she did it first. Knows she'll have to go and get another paper. She finishes what she can and goes into the kitchen. She smells the smoke from his newly lit cigarette. Puts on the coffee. Opens the kitchen window and breathes in the fresh air. Closes her eyes and dreams. He comes into the kitchen and asks for the paper. She tells him it's on the bed. The crossword's done and she doesn't want to hear about it. He sits down at the kitchen table and looks at her. She hates it when he looks at her like that. Suddenly feels all her wrinkles spring out around her eyes. She looks at him out of the corner of those eyes. Waits for the next word. He shakes his head and slaps his knee. Says something about wondering which is worse, waking up to a sore neck or waking up to her. He laughs and goes back into the living room.

The coffee fills the pot, the phone rings and she wishes it was work asking her to come in. Wishes it was a friend who's been hurt and she'll have to rush over to their house or the hospital— just wishes it was an excuse to get her out of the house. She answers and it's a survey company. She says she'll do the survey so she won't have to talk to him. He comes in, gets his own coffee. Looks at her like, *who the hell's she talking to*. She laughs a little. Hams it up. He waits by the counter. Pretends he's looking for something. She says thank you, laughs again and hangs up. He asks her who it was. She says, just a friend, then gets herself a coffee. He squints his eyes and says he didn't think she had any friends. She turns her back on him and takes a deep breath.

He gathers up the empty beer cans and leaves for his daily walk. She picks up his dirty dishes, his socks, his cigarette butts. She scratches her head and looks in the mirror. Brushes her hair out of her eyes and sucks in her stomach. Turns sideways. Thinks there might still be a figure in there somewhere. Thinks it's not too late to dig it out. Wonders about where she'll be this time next year. Dreams of being in the city, married to some businessman and possibly, just possibly, happy. She pours herself a whiskey and throws his socks away. Pours another whiskey and goes into the basement to search for old photographs. She wants to look at herself then.

She finds the box marked photographs. Easy. She pulls out a

pile marked high school. She flips over the first one and chuck-les to herself. Holds her hand over her mouth and chuckles. She keeps on going and soon she's practically howling. She stops. Goes quiet.

Looks at her silky long hair. Looks at her long thin legs, her pretty clothes, her smiles. Looks at the young girls standing around her, beside her. Wonders where they are. The ones she knew would get out of this town the first chance they had. The ones that went on to the other schools. The ones that would guarantee there's no need to come back here.

She keeps on flipping through the past. Comes to a picture of herself in the arms of a handsome boy. He's got a little smirk on his face and he's holding her from behind. Holding her tight and she's laughing like he's tickling her. Her cheeks are pink and her legs are raised up in the air. She's got her hair in pigtails and his is dark and curly and dishevelled. In the next photo, they're holding hands. Holding hands tightly and looking down. She's got her other hand over her eyes. He's gazing into the distance.

When she first saw the look of shock on his face about the baby, she thought she was going to die. Wished she'd never told him. Wished she'd left town or jumped off the bridge. She lay in her bed at night, while the rest of the house slept, contemplating all the ways out of this mess. She lay wide-eyed from sunset to sunrise. Her mum telling her for some reason it would all be all right. Her mum telling her that because she was only sixteen when she gave birth to her first child. Was it all right then?

She looks back at the pictures, back at his smiling face, back at her pigtails and pink cheeks. She wonders what would have happened if the baby had lived.

Would she be with him now? If she'd never told him would he be around now? Would he have married her like he said he would?

She thinks of her mum at her side while she lay in pain on the hospital bed. It all lasted such a short time. That pain, that love, that life. Fleeting. This is an eternity, she thinks, sitting on the basement floor, a whiskey at her side, an okay-if-I-have-to-marry-someone husband on his way back home. All stocked up with beer and nothing interesting to say.

He walks through the door and calls her name. Calls her name again. Needs her there for safety. Needs to know that even though he talks badly to her—makes her feel small and like he doesn't want her around—that he can't live without her. Can't live alone. What would he do alone?

In the silence, he panics. Starts screaming her name, throwing things around the room. Runs around the house searching for her. She sits on the cold concrete floor, listening to his hollers, to his footsteps, to his fear.

He's in his chair trembling when she comes into the room. She walks over to him and takes him in her arms. Strokes his head and whispers, everything's okay, baby, everything's okay, mummy's here.

All the Things I'd Say to
Ingmar Bergman

He throws his cigarette into the air and makes noises like a dive-bomber as it descends onto the grass. "That's okay hon," he says, "it's all blown to pieces now anyway."

He walks one way and I walk home. Realize he's got the keys. But that's okay, the front porch has always been my favourite part of the house. I want to talk to him and tell him I can't live here anymore. Can't sleep in the same bed. Can't tell him I love him and I did love him. I want to drink till the ground disappears. I sit here on my parent's hand-me-down garden furniture. I think and think about how people live in the same house together, day-in and day-out and like it. I think about who vacuums, who cooks, who walks the dogs, who gets the bathroom first in the morning, who sleeps in.

He comes around the corner with his head down. I watch him and see something I had forgotten. He looks vulnerable. I see his-lips move and wish he would talk to me as much as he talks to himself. If we could talk, maybe we could carry on. But it's too late for maybes when my mind was made up long ago. It's just a matter of getting off the front porch and into a cab.

I look back at the shattered past and breathe deeply, this new, fresh air. I open my eyes wider than they've ever been and someone new strolls in. I look, look back and look away. I hear him say something about Ingmar Bergman and laugh. I look and that's that and carry on because carrying on is easier at this point. Easier and right. I place the flowers I bought myself to brighten up the house, into a waiting crystal vase. I open the windows and turn on the radio. All songs bring new thoughts and I'm dreaming to lyrics like, "I'll take you down the only road I've ever been down." I sit on my favourite chair in the kitchen and light a cigarette, pour a drink—Cuban rum and orange juice. And I think about the-someone-new. The craziness of being drawn to a stranger by a simple thing like a laugh, a good line, a pair of eyes. And what? I shake my head, shake my head and laugh and stop laughing because one day this won't be funny. He'll be in the kitchen sitting on the other chair and I'll have to deal with him being here, real and part of my life. The part I fought so hard to get back.

I left the old neighbourhood and headed to the east side of town with all parts of my life bundled in pieces within me, and I've been piecing it all together ever since. I'm almost whole. And now I feel a twinkle in my eye and a thump in my heart and I think I should close the windows, turn out the lights and hide. But something in him is keeping my feet from running. Something.

This friend comes by and tells me I'm crazy. Tells me it's time to be alone for awhile. Tells me this is the last thing I need. I light another cigarette, pour the last drops of rum into a tall glass and say, no, this is the last thing I need. She leaves, I relax. I lie with my head at the foot of my bed and stare at the ceiling.

It's turning black and white. I'm drifting into some scene of a morbid black and white film and I think it's the *Seventh Seal*. I'm not too sure yet but I know I'll know soon. Then I realize as I walk out of the film and into a theatre that I'm back in 1957 at the opening of the *Seventh Seal* and I'm all dressed up and everyone's all dressed up, and in walks Ingmar Bergman.

People are saying things to him, saying things to him in Swedish because I've somehow gone from my bed, back to 1957 and I'm at the Swedish premiere of the *Seventh Seal* and Ingmar Bergman is getting closer to me. And all I can think about is, what am I going to say to Ingmar Bergman? What can I say to Ingmar Bergman?

He's getting closer and I'm getting warmer and colder and feeling faint, and completely and utterly at a loss for words. I'm trying to come up with something brilliant, something witty— something. He stops in front of me and I look into his eyes, hold out my hand and say, I am Death. He smiles and walks on. And I can't believe I just said that. I can't believe I just said that to Ingmar Bergman, and I want to die.

I look around and nobody's looking at me. I look around and my clothes are still piled on the chair next to my bed. My feet are on my pillows, my head at the foot of the bed. The phone rings, it's the-someone-new and I just can't bring myself to open my mouth.

The Long Gone

I love him. I love him not. I love him. I love him not.

I wait tables in the city. I think about him most nights when I get home tired and wonder if he's sleeping. He'll rise early, probably only a couple of hours after I get home and go to bed. I wonder if he thinks of me when he wakes, when he goes to sleep. I know he simply wakes and goes to sleep—thoughtless. There are times I want to pick up the phone and call. At least there were times I wanted to pick up the phone and call. I can let it go now and it helps.

I serve beer to men with no lives. Men who eat breakfast, lunch and dinner in the same bar. Pick their favourite bar not by its food or clientele, but by its waitresses. Each one has a favourite. Some have the same favourite because there are only so many per customer. My place is small. I'm one of five. I'm the quiet one, they say. I take what I get, then leave.

I've got a dog that lies at my side while I sleep. While he

sleeps, the boy, all bent over himself probably; mouth open and snoring, the dog sleeps silently, calmly with me—the loyal type. I wake sometimes in the night after a hard shift. Wake with the thought of something I've forgotten, will forget still. Wake and can't put my finger on what it was or is or will be. I just tire myself out worrying and fall back to sleep. It's a vicious circle. I never get enough sleep. Work till two, hang out till five. The free times come at odd hours and when they happen I have to make the most of them. Without me, his life drifts by in the country.

A waitress I work nights with has store-bought boobs and a diamond in her teeth. I thought it was food one day but wondered why it sparkled. I asked her about it. Why not a ruby or an amethyst, something with colour for contrast so it looks like a gem. Why a diamond? All that money to put something in a tooth that looks like a piece of food or plaque. I don't get it.

That waitress lives in a condo with an older man with money. The kind who buys dinner and nice clothes for his girl, then goes out at night while she's at home watching TV, and cheats on her with chicks he meets in bars because men with money are never satisfied. That waitress is here because she got tired of stripping. She's a nice girl, despite her choices.

I go to downtown bars sometimes with that waitress. Men fall all over her, buy her drinks, give her phone numbers. I stand a few feet away sipping the drink I bought myself.

I blush for the men out of embarrassment. She laughs and giggles and bats her eyes. Really bats her eyes. She looks down at her cleavage as much as they do. She looks around occasionally to see where I am. I kind of glance back and that's the extent of our communication. She finishes all her drinks and just as they're getting to the point where they're about to start fighting over who's going to take her home, she gives me the wide-eyed let's-go-now-look and we take off out the door. We run to the car.

She laughs and gets behind the wheel—hammered. She starts the engine, backs up into another car and drives on. I ask her if she loves the man she lives with. She says, she doesn't know. Men dream about girls like her.

Fixed

Perhaps today she'll do it. You stand, clenching your teeth, trying not to move, not to pressure her too much as she ponders the menu. The red-wine-and-a-clubhouse-on-brown lady, no mayo. Everyday since you started working there fifteen months ago. Everyday around one p.m. She has lunch with an older distinguished gentleman, gray hair, gray beard, gray suit, white shirt. And a young man, tall, pale face, thin brown hair, pale green suit—always a suit in some shade of green. Always thin. She arrives a little later than the men. Comes rushing in with windswept hair even on the calmest, windless days. Breezes in a little out of breath. Flicks her hair out of her face. Takes off her coat, her blazer. Shoves her chest across the room and her ass into the booth, bounces around a little then sits on her feet. Always sits on her feet like an over enthusiastic schoolgirl. She lights a cigarette gives you the I'm-ready-look. The no-I-don't-need-a-menu-I'll-have-the-usual look. So you go over and ask if they're ready to order and the two men look lost. She looks at them and says, I'm ready, I know what I want. You're not ready? You don't know what you want? And they stare at her, then throw their worried gazes into the menu and you say, how about a drink for now while you decide and she says, I'll have a glass of red wine and a clubhouse on brown, no mayo and fries, yeah, fries. The gray man orders a glass of red wine. The pale green man orders a Carlsberg Light in a bottle. You've already got the drinks waiting on the bar behind the taps.

Today, she comes in, they've been waiting longer than usual, already have their drinks, their menus. You say hi, and offer her a menu. She takes it. She takes it and you're astounded.

You think maybe she's taken it but hasn't really realized she's taken it. She's taken it because she's flustered. She's just whisked in and sat down and she's a little later than usual and you've walked right up to her and handed her something, and before she's had time to process what it is you've just shoved in front of her face, she grabs it. Grabs it automatically, without thinking. So you know she'll blink, realize she's just accepted a menu, and any second she's going to put it down and shove it to the other end of the table. The farthest end of the table next to the sugar and the salt and pepper because she doesn't need it. She never needs it. So you wait and you watch as she positions her feet under her ass, rocks around a bit, eyes fixed on the men in front of her, talking, getting comfortable and still holding onto the menu.

You wait. They talk and talk and the men open their menus. Open their menus and quietly look at the selection, as they always do. You serve another table, turn back around and she's sitting on her knees, feet nestled beneath her ass, head down, reading her menu. You stop dead in your tracks. You say something like Jesus, involuntarily, aloud. They close their menus and look at her. She starts bouncing slightly on her bench, getting visibly agitated. You approach slowly, very slowly and ask if they're ready to order. She tells the two men to go ahead. They make funny faces like oh, okay, because it's something they never have the opportunity of doing with her. The gray man orders a house salad with house dressing. The pale green man orders the special, the chicken on a kaiser with soup. You turn to her. Silently. She hums and haws and looks at the pale green man, bounces on her heels a little, looks at the specials board. Looks at you. You press your lips together and widen your eyes. Pen ready. You wait eagerly. Unbelievably intrigued by what she's going to order.

She looks back at the pale green man. Yeah, she says, yeah. That sounds good, but can I get it on something other than a kaiser? Like sliced bread, you say. Yeah, Yeah, she says. Or just on it's own, you offer. Oh, she says, oh I never thought of that. The possibilities are endless, the pale green man says. She looks at him stunned, afraid. Hmm, she says, uhmm, she says, OOOOH, she says. No, no, no, no, no, uhm, uhm. No, you know what. Uhm, no, you know what, I'll have a clubhouse on brown with fries no mayo. And a glass of red wine.

You stand there looking at her. You can't move. You blink a couple of times and frown. Your hand can't move the pen. Can't bring itself to jot down the order. You just stare at her and she looks up at you. Looks at the men. They shrug their shoulders. She shakes her head and looks back at you. No, you say, no. She asks you what you're talking about. Asks if there's a problem. You can't take your eyes off her. You can't move. What's the problem, she says. You tell her you're out of the clubhouse today. You don't have anymore clubhouse sandwiches. And you never will again. She furrows her brow, bounces on her ass, flicks her hair back then forth, bounces again and says oh, oh, well then, just bring me my wine.

Barred

The bartender hands the man sitting next to me a double rye and coke with a lime. I was there first. He asks me what I want and I want to tell him to serve in turn. I want to say, why'd you serve the man in the pinstripe suit and the fat wallet ahead of me when I'd clearly arrived first and had been waiting awhile. But I don't. I ask for a pint of light beer with a splash of 7-Up. It's what all my friends and I drink now. It's a way of lying to ourselves about cutting down. We drink the light stuff, water it down and drink twice as much.

The man looks over at me. I keep staring at my drink, ignoring him. He lights a cigarette and offers me one. I have my own and I show him I come prepared. He withdraws his pack and asks the bartender to suggest a good place to eat around here. The bartender tells him about Jackie's Steak House on the corner. He tells the bartender he's a vegetarian. I laugh. He asks me why I'm laughing. I guess because he seems like such a-meat-and-potatoes-kind-of-guy. I light my cigarette and say, I'm not really sure, it just struck me as funny. He asks if I know of a good vegetarian restaurant, and I tell him honestly, no, but if he checks with the hotel they'd know.

He tells me he's not staying at a hotel. He's just here for the day on business, that he's driving back to where he comes from tonight after dinner. I say, why don't you drive home now and have dinner in your own town and make things easier. He laughs and it wasn't meant to be funny. He tells me I'm bitter and that he knows my type.

Says I was probably in here drowning my sorrows over some guy. I tell him that if I was drowning my sorrows over some guy I'd have gone to a better bar and ordered a real beer. If I was drowning my sorrows over some guy, I would probably be with a friend because I'm just not that hard up to be sitting alone in a downtown bar in the middle of the afternoon crying over some guy.

He says his wife's probably at home right now doing the same thing. I say, yeah, well if I was married to the likes of you I would too. He tells me I know nothing about him and I don't. I tell him he knows nothing about me, but he figures he does, just like that—just like a man. Got it all figured out with one look and a bunch of generalizations and, boom, I'm an open book! I ask him what I do. He looks at me and ponders. He says, a nurse. A nurse. He says because despite my attitude, I'm gentle looking. Looks like I'd take care of people. Or maybe a teacher, he says. I tell him he's all wrong. I tell him I'm a brain surgeon working on my law degree and finishing my Ph.D. in philosophy as a hobby. He laughs, a little.

The bartender pours him another drink and I ask him why he's drinking so much when he's got to drive home. He says he's going to eat somewhere and that will soak up the alcohol. I tell him he's crazy, that it doesn't work that way. And what if he got into a horrible accident on the way home, his poor wife would be devastated. Then I offer to buy him another.

He says his wife is lucky to be married to a man like himself. He's successful, good-looking. She's got it made, he says. I ask if he cooks and cleans and does the grocery shopping. He says, no, that's her job. And I say, just as I thought.

I ask what his wife does and he says nothing. Then he adds, she does all that house stuff, you know all the stuff you just mentioned. He laughs and says, not all women want to work. Some women are happy being at home making men happy. I tell him, that's work.

He asks me if I'm married. I tell him no. He asks me if I've ever been married and I tell him no. He asks me if I've ever been in love and I tell him I think I am, but it's hard to tell these days. I've thought so many times that I've been in love and been wrong. I can't tell anymore. I ask him if he's in love and he says not anymore. I feel my heart sink and wonder what his wife would do if she heard him say that. If she walked through the door at that very moment and saw him sitting next to another woman and overheard him telling that other woman that he's not in love with his wife anymore. What would I do? And I think about all the men who are no longer in love with their wives that sit in bars on business trips drinking rye and coke talking to strange women. And all they really want is for that business trip to last forever so they never have to go back. So they never have to face what it is they're running away from.

I ask him if he's a salesman. He says yes. I ask him what he sells. He tells me he works for a cosmetics company. He sells makeup. He tells me men are better at selling makeup, because if a man says a colour looks great on a woman, men just love that, they'll buy it. He tells me cosmetics companies prefer to hire male salespeople. I tell him that's bullshit. Then wonder if it is.

I ask if his wife is pretty. He says sort of. I ask him if he gives her free makeup to make herself prettier. He says he doesn't like it when his wife wears makeup. Ah, I say, the old you're-pretty-enough-you-don't-need-to-wear-makeup line. Isn't that a bit hypocritical for a makeup salesman? He says, not really. But you said she's not that pretty, I say.

He says, she's pretty enough.

I light another cigarette and look at his profile as he says something to the bartender. He's got one of those square male-modellish jaws, dark brown hair that wisps down over his left eye. He's tall and a little heavy, probably from drinking too much in his twenties and now I figure he's probably in his early forties. He's attractive, a little. Probably was a lot more attractive in his youth. He's got a nice smile and relatively gentle eyes despite his attitude and pigheadedness. I bet he looks good in the right pair of jeans and a T-shirt.

The office building releases its employees for another day. The bar's filling up and in walks a woman with legs up to her chin and cheekbones with edges. She sits next to him on the other side. He notices her immediately, offers her a cigarette and she takes it.

Acrylic Dreams

Today I painted my toenails blue. Something I swore I'd never do. I did it for my mother. To relieve her fear of what people would think of her if they saw the state of my dirty, unpainted toenails. I often wonder how the state of my toenails reflects on her and never understand. Mothers think of these things. These things don't have mothers.

On my numerous walks along the beach, I see a lot of bare feet and even a boy I used to date once. I noticed he has dirty toes and when I noticed his dirty toes I didn't think, Oh my God what must his mother be like? I thought, wow, before I painted my toenails blue did my toenails look that bad? I don't date that boy anymore. Not because of his toenails, although I could use that as one of the many reasons I'm trying to convince myself that it's better this way, but because I couldn't take it anymore. His uneven temperament and in and out of like thing and his glares and his sneers and his insults. I could mention the good things because despite his bad side, he is a kind, sweet boy. He just prefers not to be that way with me just in case I stick around or stand a little closer, or think for one second that he might actually like me.

When I painted my fingernails blue, I was astonished by how many boys, not the ex-boy, noticed and complimented my nails. I never used to paint my fingernails either. I only grew my fingernails to bite them. But one day my nails just started growing. And they are strong. They rarely break. And when I was making concessions for my mother by painting my toenails, I looked at my fingernails and I thought, hmmm, they're really quite long and shapely. I should paint them too. They're not dirty like my toes and, unlike my toes, painted fingernails don't frighten me.

Since I've been painting my nails blue, I'm amazed by what boys notice and what boys don't. Like a girl's incredible personality, talent and beauty seem to go unnoticed by certain boys. Whereas, when she stretches her unheld hands toward her drink or her cigarette they instantly turn wide-eyed and say, "Wow, look at your nails. They're blue. Nice. That's sexy." Amazing. All these years of wondering what makes them tick. Whether it's a girl's confidence, her charm, her laugh, her legs, her breasts, her eyes, her mind. Then I think, what would they do if I took off my shoes? What would they think of my mother?

Double Diamond

I remember nights in agony. I remember too-many Double Diamonds and Players cigarettes. I remember hanging my head low to reach hers and it reached hers too late. The lady next door came to me one night and held my hand—said she'd try to understand.

There were nights, I swear, I sat in my backyard and watched her bedroom light. She was up and she seemed always up and I wondered, is this right? She spoke broken English. She came from a hot place in Europe. I asked her why she left and she said for a husband and a shot at something new. I knew it cost her twenty-five years working in a pickle factory for a man that needed her, but didn't love her. His first wife, his only love, had passed away and she knew she could never be that dead woman—as long as she lived.

I caught her in tears—once. She was exhausted. Had cooked and canned tomatoes all night. She was beautiful when she cried. I can't deny the strange love I felt for her. She drove me crazy really, couldn't stand her, till I saw her tears, then she was different. I had to love her when I saw her insides slide down her cheeks at dawn.

She was petrified of dogs except my dog. She loved my dog. She called her Katarina though her name was Skye. Said Skye was a boy's name. I said no, Skye's a Scottish name. She's named after the Isle of Skye and she didn't understand, just called her Katarina.

She threw her tennis balls and fed her too much white bread and mango, felt protected by the dog. She was scared of everything. Thought she would be hurt by some burglar. But Skye, Katarina, would save her. We all wanted Skye to save us. She had too many people depending on her—for such a young dog.

The lady next door banged on my door too early for reasons. Gave me cookies I couldn't eat and hot peppers which I loved. Her husband came and went. She walked on swollen feet and complained about the cold and the heat and the rain and the snow and how she missed her family back home. My father spoke to her in her mother tongue. I said he was Italian in his last life. She didn't understand. She said he was handsome for his age but had no idea of his age. She gave him tomatoes and offered him homemade wine. He doesn't drink wine. Said my mother was beautiful—and she is—and wondered how my mother put up with me. The girl who seemed to be home too much during the day and cried aloud in her backyard at all hours of the night and lied about it to the lady next door, who'd been watching her in the middle of the night when they both should have been sleeping. They both should have been sleeping beside the men that should be watching out for them. The men that kept them up.

From the In Side

I'm sitting in a small dimly-lit Italian coffee shop. The place is empty and the only other customer has just walked in and sat down beside me. I'm a little relieved to no longer be the only patron, but disturbed by her choice of seats. I ignore her discretely. I lower my head deep into an entertainment weekly and sip uncomfortably on my tea. Every sound I make is amplified. A sip is a slurp, a swallow a gulp, a breath an effort.

She orders quickly, then looks at my tea.

"Is that all you live on", she asks. I'm a little surprised by her forwardness. But, how surprised can I be by a stranger who sits down beside me in an empty café. I look at her questioningly, head tilted to one side and furrow further my already furrowed brow. She persists, "what do you live on?"

I feel compelled to answer. I look into my teacup and say, "hopes, dreams and Tylenol extra strength."

She says, "I know a woman who stays up all night so she can

sleep through the days. I can see her jogging on the spot in her room at three a.m."

I look at her skeptically as she speaks half to me and half to her bowl of something hot and frothy in front of her. And I'm wondering why these things happen to me; always being stopped and asked for directions when I'm in a hurry, ambushed by Bible-thumpers, and turned to for answers by strangers. If I could be anything I would be invisible.

"I don't think I'm as bad as her," she continues. "The times when my brain locks and I can't think the thoughts I want are the worst. That's when I remain immobile for days and try to empty it of conventionality. A mind can only take so much you know, like a stomach."

Smiling's the only fitting reaction at the moment. My palms are sweating. I can feel the hair growing out of my head and I'm shaking slightly. To open my mouth could be dangerous; I might begin conversing with her, revealing a secret or two, agreeing with her. I don't want that.

I felt like I did in grade school when I was sent to the guidance counselor. I hadn't spoken for a week and my teachers were beginning to worry. Reluctantly, I went. I sat there while she asked me unanswerable questions, as people in positions of authority are wont to do. I sat there mute.

Eventually, the counselor got frustrated and began to tell me about her traumatic upbringing. I sat in front of her smiling and trembling. She went on and on about three failed marriages, how she ran over the family dog and her recurring nightmare about hairdressers.

I had to give in and speak, to ask if I could be excused. Between sniffs, she nodded her head. I left abruptly, made it into the bathroom and vomited. Of course, she was credited with psychologically luring my voice back. Of course.

"I find mine both go at the same time," she says.

"What." I snap. She's confused me. I've responded out of frustration, or maybe she's psychologically lured me into conversation.

"My stomach and my mind, when I can't think, I can't eat. Suddenly the saying, you are what you eat makes sense to me."

Now I really can't say a word. What could anyone say to that? Except maybe the woman who jogs in her room all night.

"It's a painful draining process unplugging the mind," she sighs, looking straight into me.

"Yeah, well, that's when the Tylenol really helps," I say.

She gazes miserably out of the window. Sniffing every so often but not crying, which is a relief. My own tears don't frighten me. I cry for fun. I cry because I can't help it. I just cry. But other people's tears are different. They move me.

"When I was young I thought about suicide all the time," she says, still staring blankly at the street. "But now I like to read about other people's instead. It curbs my appetite for it."

I flip through the pages of my paper and wonder why I'm not leaving.

"Once I had a dream that I was in an old department store," she continues. "It was painted white. Everything was white. I was on the second floor with a group of people. We were on an ornate balcony. There was a crowd of people below seated in a semi-circle looking up at us. I was with a boy. We were at the very edge of the balcony and he had a rope around his neck. A woman walked over to me and tried to put a rope around mine. I struggled, but deep inside I wanted her to. The boy stood up and leapt over the edge of the balcony. He dangled like a fish on the end of a fishing line. The crowd gasped, then looked up at me. The rope was now around my neck. Part of me wanted so badly to jump. Part of me wanted to live. The people behind began pushing me closer and closer to the edge. I jumped, but I didn't die. The rope was long enough that I landed on my feet. I didn't die. Can I have another cappuccino please?"

The waitress brings her another fancy coffee and more hot water for my tea. I hadn't asked but I guess some things go without saying.

"Now I lay me down to sleep. I pray the Lord my soul to keep. What comes next?" She asks.

I don't know so I don't answer. The only prayer I used to say was God bless ma and pa, and so on and so on. I suppose that isn't even a prayer.

Now, when I feel really desperate, I say please God make the phone ring, or please God don't let him be out with another woman, or please God let this day be over.

I was taken to Sunday school by a friend once. I never forgave her. I went to church once—when a friend got married. I tried reading the Bible once. I read two pages and threw it across the floor. It's the only book I didn't finish. Please God don't let this woman ask me any more religious questions.

"My son always asked me what came next," she says. " I'd forget, so I'd make things up. He'd repeat what I'd say, without question. One night, I went into his bedroom. He was sitting at his desk writing. I asked him what he was doing and he said he was writing a list of things the Lord could do with his soul, so that I wouldn't have to make up new things every night. Now when I go to sleep I look at his list and pray the Lord is looking after his soul in at least one of those ways." She puts her head in her hands and goes all quiet.

I don't know what to do, so I gaze out the window.

It's amazing how you can sit indoors for hours and watch the world pass by outside. You can sit motionless for hours but life itself doesn't stop. That was always one of the paradoxes about school. I used to sit at my desk day after day learning about life as it passed me by. The only things I learned in school were how to dream effectively and that to learn about life is to live it from the outside in, not from the inside out. We were always learning about things that had been, not things that are or were about to be.

Some of my schoolmates became lawyers, doctors and accountants. They lead their textbook existences but what do they know about life.

"They still try to comfort me by saying it wasn't my fault," she resumes, "that I have to stop blaming myself. All the psychiatrists in the world can't ease your conscience about losing a child. I've never been to one, but that's what I think."

A small insect makes its way across the table. Both our eyes are on it. You are a brave one, I think. Are we as brave for venturing out of our houses in a day?

I had a friend who was married to a woman who was afraid to leave her house. She went to a psychic to find out if something had occurred in a past life that had manifested itself in her psyche. The psychic told her that she had lived hundreds of years ago. She'd been a man. A Chinese man. The town in which he lived was in the midst of political unrest. He left for work as usual one day. When he returned at the end of the day his house had been burned to the ground, and his wife and children had been killed. He never forgave himself for not being there to save them, for not being there when they needed him most. He never forgave himself.

She flattens the insect with her thumb.

"I suppose in the long run all this worrying won't have been worth it." She sighs. Nothing comes from worrying. It's counterproductive. It's like the words 'should have'. To say 'I should have done this' or 'I should have done that' is a waste of time.

The fact is, it's been done. Move on. Don't do it again. 'Should' should be abolished, Don't you think?"

I nod my head slightly.

How do you stop worrying. I worry about worrying. Sometimes when I'm sleeping, I'm awakened by waves of worry moving from my toes to my head in a constant swaying motion. Just like waves gliding onto shore. I feel seasick. How do you stop waves from coming to shore? How do you stop worrying? My ma says I'm thin from worry. That soon I'll be able to see my worries from the lines on my face. They'll all be spelled out for everyone to read by the lines on my face. Good, I think. Then maybe someone will read one and offer some advice. I suppose if you keep all your worries inside they eventually surface in one way or another. They say it's not good to keep things inside. But you don't want to let them out to just anybody.

"Some days come and go like a glass of warm milk, bland but soothing." She says. " They put me to sleep. Others are gritty like eating sand. Just like taking a handful of sand and shoving it into your mouth, grinding your teeth then swallowing. Can you feel it? Yesterday was like that."

She speaks to the window. It doesn't really matter if I respond or not. Even when she asks me questions she doesn't really wait for an answer. She reminds me of David from the book *The Chrysalids*.

The part when his uncle says, "Wouldn't it be more fun to do your chattering with some of the other kids? More interesting than just sitting and talking to yourself." And David says, "but I was."

The reflection of the amber traffic light beats against the window. Flashing off and on, cars break cautiously at its command.

The noise from the street reverberates against the silence in here. The occasional clacking of dishes comes from the kitchen, a sneeze and a cough but not a word. Too uncomfortably silent to move.

She lifts her head up. Stretches her neck so that her hair

touches the nape of her back and reaches her hands toward the ceiling, as if she's reaching for something. As if something's calling to her. I roll my eyes toward the ceiling, examine it thoroughly and wait to be amazed. There's nothing but flies congregating around the lights. Flying menacingly around and around and around. Dizzy and disappointed I look at her, startled to find her looking back at me.

"What are you staring at?" she taunts.

"Nothing," I say, caught off guard. "The flies."

I throw my eyes back into the paper, scrunch my nose and sigh through it like a miffed little bull. A cool breeze circulates around the table. A dead fly drops abruptly, intrusively on the page in front of me. I shiver, then turn to find myself all alone.

Who Die

They led me into room after room. There was always another stranger asking questions I've never asked myself. At first it was awkward, jarring, like the sight of painted toenails. Some things aren't meant to be painted.

No, I wasn't touched in strange places as a child. Not beaten. Just born. It's the only thing I can think to blame it on. It's my feet that hurt the most after all this. From all the running. One more mile, I'd say, one more mile. Although I had no way of measuring distance. I was guessing, always guessing.

Blue sheets. The hospitals all had blue sheets. Baby blue. Almost baby blue—not so gentle. That and tulips. In the window. On the bedside table. Tulips. Who was sending me tulips everywhere I went?

The doctor, perhaps; he had that glint in his eye every time he smiled at me. He thought I was paranoid because I rarely looked into his eyes. I was avoiding the glint.

The nurse. Maybe it was the nurse. She swore she'd never forget me, wherever I went. Told me I was special, lovely—a flower.

I sit trembling in locked quarters as the last of the young girls dressed in red and white, places three pills into my hand, smiles the little smile they do without looking into my eyes, and backs away. I don't belong here, I tell her. She doesn't understand.

I don't belong here, I say, when the blinds are lifted, come morning, by the man in the white coat. Now, now, he says, too much freedom would go to your head. And he's gone before I have time to ask him if they've found what they're looking for.

It was when I looked up into the deserted sky that I felt the whole world fall out from beneath my feet. You can't stay here all night, he said, that cowboy, horse and all; cowboy hat and a twang.

You've got to be kidding, I said, I live here.

In the desert?

Oh yes, I said, all over.

You don't belong here, he said.

Oh, but I know, I said. That's what I tried to tell the doctor.

I never saw that cowboy again.

Little Devils in Blue Jeans

It didn't hurt like I thought it would. Like it did the first time and the second time. It's a good morning, this morning. This stretching across the width of the bed and not touching something else. Touching nothing but space and having nothing but time. Alone at last and not hurting from the silence.

A voice told me this is all wrong and I carried on and carried on despite the screams and the tears and the shaking of everybody else's head but mine—mine and his. This I think about over tea with my dog at my feet letting me know he'll always be here, this morning and every morning till one of us ceases to exist.

The other girl who lives in this house calls from work and asks me how I am. I say fine. It's all okay now. He pushed me too far. The one last push you need to shove them out of the tunnel and into the light and it's all so clear and obvious, and the delusion that this could ever have been more is in tiny pieces on the ground. And when I saw him yesterday without the costume, out of character, he was just the skin and bones of someone I had only dreamt up once. It's amazing what we create. Did it even really happen? I wonder now that he hasn't called to see if I'm all right, just to say anything.

She says her boy's taking her out tonight. She's on the brink of walking away, but is still making excuses. Still hoping it'll change. After tonight, she'll decide. I listen and know tonight will bring her home in tears and tomorrow will be spent waiting for the phone to ring and making more excuses.

I tell her I made the right decision too late. I don't miss him like I did the first time or the second time. She tells me it's better this way. I know it is. I noticed the colour of the sky this morning. I noticed my dog's eyes are even more caring than I remembered. I noticed yesterday I had a better conversation with my friend's nine-year-old son about books and planets and spirits than I'd ever had with him.

Same Old Story

The unreliable one shows up at the house with roses and good intentions. I let him in cautiously and ask if he wants tea. He always wants tea. It's one thing I can rely on. He lights a cigarette and smiles a sort of half-smile. The one used when a confession is about to be told. I brace myself. I close my ears, try not to read his lips then nod my head when his lips stop moving and his eyes stare at the floor. Then I shake my head like every word he said was unbearable to hear. I think, it doesn't matter what he's just said. It doesn't matter that I didn't hear a word of it. It's all the same after awhile and I won't react like he thought I would and he'll be relieved. We'll carry on and drink tea.

He wonders why I still talk to him after all this. I wonder too. We love all the wrong people and do all the wrong things and this is just the way it is. I tell him it makes me laugh to know that no matter how much you think you've learned, no matter how well you think you know the road, there's always another hole to fall into. The only difference is the depth and the width and now I've noticed some have ladders. That's new.

And the other thing, I tell him, is that no matter how much you try and fight human nature, your choices are limited. Why you're emotionally attracted to someone or physically attracted to someone is beyond your control—and that sucks. He listens and nods his head and I wonder if he's listening or has already tuned me out like I do to him. But I'm not telling him anything he doesn't know or won't eventually know as time goes by.

I'm telling him everything I need to hear and whether or not he was here, I'd still be drinking tea, and having this conversation with myself.

The unreliable one sits on the edge of his seat. Impatience filling up his cup as the tea's being drained out. I can see he's thinking of exit lines, quickly, before I say something that he might have to answer to. Before I say something truthful about how I feel about him. You can never say how you really feel, remember. Just skirt around the issues, drink more tea, laugh about something stupid you did at work last night, smoke a cigarette even though you quit. If you want to keep him around a bit longer, just bullshit. He won't mind, it's what he prefers.

I notice his hair has grown since the last time I saw him and his eyes seem bigger—somehow. His dark skin's smoother despite the tattoo of the devil on his left arm. He's told me things about himself that make me want to back away from him into another room and cry. It makes me want to run away from all the wrong in this world. The injustices and the pain inflicted on people by mothers and fathers that crush the hopes and dreams and bones of the children they brought into this world supposedly because of love. It makes me want to crawl beneath his skin and hold every part of him till it doesn't hurt anymore. But it will always hurt no matter how much I try to take it all away. There is nothing I can do. And I know, despite the fact that he came here today bearing gifts, it's the same old story—same old song. There is nothing I can do.

Green

Things don't change much these days. All tall buildings and streams of expressionless faces. Cold. I've got a briefcase clutched under my arm. New shoes. I'm hopping in the next cab and it's taking me to the place I sit in till the sun goes down, hitting letters on a keyboard. Spelling out words I don't really understand. Answering phones and taking messages. All day.

And today, especially, I'm thinking about the night in the playground. Swinging my way into tomorrow. The moon full. Singing Gram Parson's songs at the top of my lungs for you. You sitting on the steps with a beer, listening to the boy I was with tell you war stories. You listened patiently and watched me, swinging and singing and I felt so free and so trapped. As long as my feet weren't touching the ground, up here in the air, I could love anyone I wanted. And it wasn't wrong. As soon as I set foot on the sand, I'm with the war-story-boy again. I swung for hours. The next day my muscles ached.

The boy I was with isn't with me now. And you are out of bounds, across the fine line. The playground's in your backyard, the ball in your court, every cliché in town. I can't come anywhere near you. Can't pick up the phone and call. Can't do anything at all. I can think of nothing but you and his words engraved in my head, I understand, I understand just stay away from my best friend.

The wind is chilling as I stand outside smoking. It makes me consider quitting smoking.

I walk to the park at lunch. Sit and watch the road. The ducks bore me now. I watch for an automobile. The one that you drive. The one I've discovered that one in every three people drives. But I know what makes yours different. The side door opens on the passenger side not the driver side, not both sides like the smaller vans. And you corrected me quickly one night when I called it a mini-van. It's not a mini-van you said. A midi-van then, I said because it doesn't quite strike me as maxi-van. You looked at me in the rear-view mirror. I was far enough away from you. You were adamant. I have counted over five hundred vans in your colour since last week. Very few have sliding doors on the passenger side and writing above the wheel on the driver side. I cannot recall what make. Ford. Plymouth. Plymouth is one of the most popular makes. But you don't strike me as a Plymouth kind of guy. But I could be wrong. I don't know you that well. I just remember it was warm and comfortable and green.

> If I had a Green Automobile
>   I'd go find my old companion
>   in his house on the Western ocean.
>   Ha! Ha! Ha! Ha! Ha!

I'd honk my horn at his manly gate,
inside his wife and three
    children sprawl naked
    on the living room floor.

He'd come running out
    to my car full of heroic beer
    and jump screaming at the wheel
    for he is the greater driver

—Allen Ginsberg

Once I thought I heard your engine pull up behind me as I approached my home. It was nothing.

The day drags on and I finish nothing. My boss asks me for my time card and I tell him I lost track of time a long time ago, grabbed my coat and walk home. I wondered if I kept walking west to the ocean, you might pass me on your way home. On your way home from where I don't know. I don't know what it is you do. Some say nothing, some say write, some say sales. I didn't ask you. Maybe I didn't want to know. All I know is you have stories, a lot to tell, a history. A neat house, your artwork strewn across its walls, a boat, and a green automobile.

You have a pair of Armani glasses and nice shoes. You only drink a specific type of wine—one I like. You listen to gypsy music and country music and some of your heroes are mine. You are quiet and tall and have some kind of mind. What kind of mind? Are you troubled? Sedated? Satisfied? Relieved? Worn out? Wise? Humble? Weary?

Tell me if you can hear me now, walking at the side of the road. One I'm not supposed to be walking down. Asking you what it is you're thinking. If you think of me at all. Of the night we drank bourbon till we couldn't stand, swam naked in the lake, drove the boat to an abandoned island and did what? What did we do? Did we talk? We didn't stop talking for two days after that. The boy I was with, his head in comic books, mine in the clouds, yours beneath your cowboy hat staring out at the water. The deep water we defied drunkenly the previous night. And survived.

I've come to some crossroad, don't know which way to turn. A thousand green automobiles driving by. None with the sliding door on the passenger side, with the writing above the wheel on the driver side—none with you behind the wheel.

This is My Life

The rain fell and I thought this is it. The last fall. The droning thunder of pouring rain. The splash of cars whizzing through puddles and I'm at the bus stop without an umbrella thinking this would be fine if it were twenty degrees warmer.

It's a cold November morning. The bus is already ten minutes late on account of the weather. The days when you think it would be early, sympathetically. But somehow a big thing like a bus is affected by a little thing like rain and just can't make it to the stops on time. Understandably it can't go as fast on the wet roads. It's hazardous. It should simply begin its run earlier. Leave the garage at least ten minutes earlier. But bus drivers don't think of these kinds of things. And I wished I smoked because I'm told that as soon as you light a cigarette the bus comes. And of course nobody else at this bus stop appears to smoke either. We wait and I wonder about what's at the end of the ride anyway. Why am I enduring the rain and the cold to board a bus that takes me to a place with too many flights of stairs to climb to sit behind a desk for eight hours thinking about the outside, and tall glasses of beer. I wonder why I get up early, skip breakfast, run to the bus stop; often in the rain, wait, contemplate taking up smoking, wait some more, arrive late to work, aggravated and sit bored for eight hours. This is my life.

I think of the paycheque at the end of the month. It's big and it gets me nice clothes and groceries. It pays for my nice apartment. It furnished my nice apartment. It pays for a stocked wine rack and tall glasses of beer. It pays for nights out on the town, films; and films aren't cheap these days.

It could support a drug habit if I happened to be a drug addict, which I'm not, but could be if I so desired. I could even have a car and wouldn't have to wait for stupid buses in the rain, but I don't like driving in the city. It could pay for a small house in the country so I could drive my car. If I lived in that small house in the country with my car, I wouldn't work at this job in the city and if I didn't work at this miserable job in the city, I couldn't have the house in the country or the car or the clothes. I'd be homeless and sleeping in bus shelters. I'd be free.

My clothes are soaking. My hair's soaking. I'm shivering from the cold. The cold thoughts. The thought of the cold reception I'll receive walking through the door, wet and late and unreceptive to the glares and the cold shoulders. Colder than mine. I'll drag mud through the reception area. Leave a pool of water at my feet. Ruin the new carpet. They'll make me pay. Deduct it from my great big paycheque and wait for me to show signs of caring. They'll give me extra work, make me stay late. They'll have office luncheons at my favourite restaurants and leave me to answer the phones and bring back leftovers so I can smell the food and wish I had been there. I'll tell them nobody called when all the calls they were expecting came in.

I'm starting to sneeze and shiver more. It's too late to turn back. I run to the variety store on the corner. Buy a small pack of cigarettes—menthols—because I don't know any better. Stand just inside the door to light the cigarette, look up and watch the bus go by.

This is my life.

The New Dead

When I walked past the gravestones, the first time in the rain, I didn't feel the presence of angels. I didn't hear the haunting staccato of chamber music marching through time-blackened stones. I heard rain. I watched crows land on headstones and watch me. Let me walk right up to them and ask them who they are. They don't give away secrets, these crows.

I watched my mother and father search for dead poets in the rain for me. And I thought how many parents would search for dead poets in the cold rain in Paris for their daughters. How many would and wouldn't give up till they found the likes of Rimbaud for me and take pictures of me placing stones on his grave?

Up and down and up and down we walked. In and out of nameless graves, stranger's graves, soldier's graves. I cried at the foot of Samuel Beckett. I pondered at the foot of Simone DeBeauvoir and Sartre. Wondered which one was on top. Wondered why after everything he put her through she still wanted to be buried with him. I gave her more roses than him. I almost took his back.

I felt the presence of something unsettled in the oldest part of the cemetery. I told my mother something's looming here. She told me not to tell her things like that. We jumped when the thunderous cloud of crows dispersed in the air in front of us. I looked over my shoulder and rubbed my chilly arms.

I told my mother I always believed I had the ghost of some dead writer in me. I told her that I hoped it wasn't the ghost of Edgar Allan Poe. She laughed and we laughed and happened upon the breathtaking tomb of Abelard and Héloïse. I grabbed the bars that enclosed it. In disbelief I stared at the sculptures of their bodies lying side by side in stone. Together forever their bones, their dust, their legacy, here before me. I felt smaller than time. I looked around at the dead surrounding me. The history. I felt inconsequential and that they were so much more alive than me. I looked at my mother who created me. I stood amongst the dead with the woman who gave me life and thought of all the times I tried to give it back. I thought of the summer I read the story of Abelard and Héloïse and thought I will never know love like that. I sat on a bench at the foot of true love, a mother's love and disappeared.

Sandbox

This is about dolls—heartless dolls. A neurotic Barbie lost her Ken and can't find the strength to get back in her little Barbie Corvette without running over a few of her friends on the way. I think this is all a bad joke. Must be. I'm too smart for this. Grown up girls don't act like neurotic Barbies with drinking problems and bad hair days. Nothing's perfect for the fucked-up plastic girls down the road. Not like they think it should be.

I'm thinking maybe tomorrow, I'll pack up my things in all the carrying bags I own and take my dog and me to America. Get a job in a little bistro on 52nd Street and try not to let myself get to know anyone too well. I don't want to know what some Barbie thinks of the man I'm sleeping with or how she just wants to find someone to fuck because that's the cure she needs to get over the one that she was supposed to have babies with. Baby, I don't even want to know her last name.

I want to forget the night Barbie broke up with Ken and in a rage told me in a crowded bar that the boy I'm dating fooled around with her room-mate in the park behind their house, in the sandbox. She told me this as a favour to me just after I broke the news to her that we were back together. Giving it the let's try again bit, pick up the pieces and erect a monument we can be proud to call our own. I told her this and she told me that, and I felt my bones break into tiny pieces one by one and clatter to the ground and I was afraid strangers would step on my disintegrating body and pummel it to dust. I'd have to wait until the bar cleared and attempt to sweep myself up and find a way home.

I cried the whole way home. Stayed up till sunrise and slept all the next day. Dreamt of bohemian coffee shop encounters with dishevelled-hair writers who talk sweet to me and blow cigarette smoke in my face because they think it's sexy. They're harmless and have sweet smiles and they don't drink alcohol, just coffee, because the last thing they want to do is numb their minds. Sweet.

She calls and wakes me. Yells at me for leaving a mean message on her answering machine. I'd forgotten I'd done that. She told me she regretted telling me, and did it because she's my friend. My insides contort. I'm tired of the lies and the misconceptions. The teenage sagas burrowing their way into my grownup psyche. This is like falling with bare knees onto a rock ledge. Sharp-edged-stone. This is her demise not mine.

I hang up. Lie flat on my back. Exhausted. Palms turned up. Eyes wide open. Thinking I'm in exactly the right position for death. My brain's going to shove itself through my skull any second with its relentless pounding. It's banging its way through. And I think of her. I hold my stomach. It needs to be warm. I feel the sickness that accompanies sadness and letdown—deceit.

I remember the first time I cried over a boy. The first time I felt this. This hollow cave. This emptiness and pain behind my eyes, beneath my skin. I think there is no way of knowing what someone tells you is true, all that matters is what you decide to believe.

I want to believe that tomorrow I'll be in a small bistro on 52nd Street. I'll be coming and going in new shoes. I'll have left behind the kids in the park, kissing each other when the sun goes down and the bars close; kissing each other because no one else was there that night. I want to believe that she will stop trying to make other people's lives as miserable as her own. I'm hoping my head will stop pounding.

Even if I wake up here tomorrow, this will matter little. I tell him, I'm sorry he got dragged into this. That she's trying to blame him because girlfriends are all good, and boyfriends are all bad. That this isn't about him—or us.

Forgive Me Someone For
I Have Sinned

You arrived at the church doorstep one night to confess your infidelity. You apologized for arriving so late but you couldn't go one more night without sleep, dodging you husband's caresses and God's eyes. The priest's words, whiskeyed and hot, warmed your ears, *it's never too late to say you're sorry*. You said the worst part is you're not sorry, but someone had to know. And it sure as hell wasn't going to be your husband because that would just cause all sorts of trouble. As long as God knows, you're off the hook. The priest was silent and you thought it was from disgust and disappointment and that he was speechless this time. So you sat there in the half-dark in the full-silence and you waited. Then he snored and you couldn't believe your confessions of lying and cheating and a lack of remorse put him to sleep. You woke him to say goodbye. Left without an answer, without a ticket home and split town.

You and your motorcycle-boy dreams are roaring you down

the highway and out of there fast before they come after you for another confession, another marriage, another baptism. You're finished walking through its doors and you know you'll be missed, you were its best customer. The priest's reason for unlocking its doors most days.

Your children are too big to care. As big as adults now and married—both of them—to doctors. Two kids each and cars and houses with nice furniture and they never had anything to do with you anyway. Not since your third marriage, no children luckily since your second and no more grandchildren as of yet. They never let you see the grandchildren. Because grannies on motorbikes are supposed to be a joke, not real. Because the grandchildren will grow up before you. You got tired of the insults and the shaking fingers and now you're on the highway heading for redemption in the direction of your own ma. Sweat dripping down your face. Eyes stuck on the horizon. Just keep looking forward, you're saying over and over to yourself. Just keep looking forward and ignore the faces of the men you left. They'll wonder for a few days. They'll get the scoop from the priest, they'll tell the children. Well, the husband will tell the children. Then the husband will probably have words with the other man and the other man will stand wide-eyed, jaw dropped to his knees because he didn't know you were married. You told the other man a lot of things. You left that out. It would have just caused problems.

The wind dies down after six. Traffic becomes sparse. The calm comes and the quiet. You're holed up in a little roadside motel for the night. Picked up some bourbon and a six-pack, ice and cigarettes. You're all set. You sit on the little back patio attached to your room and listen to the hum of the occasional big rig heading somewhere. You look at your hands. No rings. You never liked jewellery anyway. Only put the damn things on the days you had to—the wedding days.

You look at your withered hands still reaching out for something. Not just the glass of bourbon on the table, not the cigarette. You think about maybe calling the husband. Asking him to meet you in the next town. Out here alone on the highway, you think maybe, just maybe, you screwed up. If the priest or God didn't get to him first, you might still have a chance to redeem yourself.

Then you think about where you're going. Where are you going? And why are you always so reluctant to take someone with you. Always running away alone. But you never run back. Once you're gone, you're gone and there's something to be said for that. Surely. Another beer and you pick up the phone. You hang up the phone and go to sleep.

By morning you're a little beaten down. Can't tell if it's yesterday or tomorrow, just hope it's not today. The maid knocks on the door and you tell her you'll make your own bed.

Bewildered

The man in the cowboy hat and the cigarette dangling from his mouth tells you to watch out for the snapping turtles. You look at him like he's mad. You can't see his eyes through his thick black sunglasses, but you can imagine the red veins behind them. You can't see the things he's seen, but you've read about them in books, seen them in movies. The ones about the boys who pound too much junk into their veins, and steal from their friends, and lose their wives and go mad — then die. They all tell the same tale.

You look at your feet beneath the water every few seconds for snapping turtles. He's got you worried now. Even though you know the most dangerous thing in these waters might be a thirty pound pike and you only learned last week that pike grow that big and can be aggressive. But it's the afternoon and you're not likely to have one swimming between your legs and suddenly turn around and bite you. In fact there's nothing close to you that's alive or dangerous, except for the man in the cowboy hat and the cigarette dangling from his mouth who just sits there looking in your direction. You can't tell exactly what he's looking at cause of his sunglasses, but his head's facing you and you're barely dressed except for a bathing suit; hair long and wet floating behind you. And you have no idea when he last saw a woman.

He lives here in the wilderness, summer and winter. Just him and his dog. The gray and white dog: glimmering fangs and yellow eyes, sitting at the man's feet watching you. At best you can see his eyes. You can't escape. But he doesn't frighten you. Just makes you wonder. And why you come to this part of the lake to swim still amazes you when you know he'll be here. His dog will be here.

But you're accustomed to these waters. Been swimming in this part of the lake since you were a child and a teenager and now an age neither here nor there. And it was here you always came to escape the family and the other families's sons who were your age and younger, who wouldn't give you any peace. Especially when your body took shape and you threw in your one-piece for a bikini. Even the newly applied mascara running down your face didn't put them off. They never let up. So you dove in one day and they thought, you never came up.

You heard them screaming for your mother, for their mother's. You swam that whole afternoon alone on the other side of the lake and patted yourself on the back. You had no idea you could hold your breath that long. You swam the width of that lake every day you could. Your mother in on your secret after crying that whole afternoon at the thought of your demise. She slapped you that day, but she kept your secret all other days.

The boys forgot and moved on. You scared them once and that was it for their interest in you. You learned a lot about boys that day. The man with the cowboy hat and the cigarette dangling from his mouth wasn't there in the beginning. He just came around one summer, years later when you came to the other side of the lake out of habit, not escape because no one was left to escape from.

You were scraping your fingers through the sand at the bottom of the lake, in silence and peace. You glided up and saw the rippling reflection of a man standing on the end of the dock looking down at you. You popped your head through the water. He jumped back and walked away. Didn't look back. You watched him disappear into the woods, a dog at his heels. You dried yourself off and sat and waited for him to return. He didn't return and you held your breath, dove into the water and swam home. Sat up all night, eyes peeled on the window. Ears open. Wide open. Nothing.

When you met again, his cigarette smoke reached you before him. You heard his footsteps on the dock, his dog clicking along beside him. You didn't turn around. You pretended you didn't hear him. You wiped your wet hair off your shoulders. He stopped and stood behind you. You waited and finally when you couldn't take it anymore, you turned around. He held out a glass to you. Didn't say a word just held out a glass half-full of some golden liquid with a kind of half-smile leaning on his troubled face. The dog gave you his paw.

Keeping it All in Tune

She picks up the battered acoustic guitar in the corner by the fireplace. She starts singing like a chorus of angels. Picking strings not touched in years. Somehow she's keeping it all in tune. I know I'm not supposed to ask but I want to ask what her husband was really like when his hands strummed those strings. Was it true he took pills a handful at a time, with chasers of bourbon or whiskey or whatever he could get his hands on? Her boys told me, he found her in a rundown southern bar singing to bikers and age-old waitresses.

One night, he kissed her gently and promised to take her away from the two-bit bar and its vast emptiness. She believed him. She was young. Then she was pregnant, then married. He kept singing and travelling and pill-popping and trying to save them and trying to save himself. She kept hanging on and hanging on. He let go.

She's dancing barefoot across the room in a small flowered

dress, revealing her thin, agile legs. Her three boys carry on their conversation unfazed like she was the evening breeze. I don't want to stare but I can't take my eyes off her porcelain skin. Her silver hair flowing down her child-like body. She's in her own world, eyes closed, smiling like she's dreaming about a man. The man she lost. Dead before he really was a man. And I wonder what she did with that love, because she can't resurrect the dead no matter how much she tries and I suppose she keeps going through life alone because she thinks there will never be another man like him.

She asks me to sing along with her and I'm so nervous. My voice is like a baby rooster's. Hers is like velvet. I'll just listen I tell her and she frowns. She hums a few bars, puts down the guitar and says the spirit's gone.

She tells me she's cutting her visit short. I tell her I'm sorry if it was something I did or didn't do. She brushes her hand across my own and smiles. The boys try to convince her to stay. Keep looking at me for some kind of explanation and truly I can't think of what to say. I wouldn't sing with her and now I've driven her away. They just look at me like I'm leaving something out.

I walk down by the water and put my toes in. It's not too cold now that the summer's been here for so long. Soon it'll be covered in ice and I'll only be able to touch its surface. She sits down next to me and shoves her feet in the water. I can't remember the last time I swam, she tells me, been afraid of the water since he died. I keep looking at the water. She keeps talking.

She says there's not a day goes by she doesn't think of him. She's wondering if maybe one day, when she's playing one of his songs, he'll just appear. Pick up on the next verse and she'll fall back in harmony.

It's been years and it hasn't happened, but she keeps singing.

She tells me she never loved anyone again like she loved him and wonders if that's because he left before that love had time to run out. She says, sometimes it's too hard to look at the boys. Every one of them has his eyes. Wished she never had them now that they all remind her too much of him. And I think, isn't that the way it's supposed to be? I tell her I love her boys because they are so much like her. She says the one I love most is the one that has become the spitting image of his father. The one who's eyes frighten her. The one she can't reach because she feels safer at a distance. I tell her I'll never leave him. She tells me it's his leaving that worries her.

Everybody's Slave

She's walking down the middle of the boulevard with a half empty bottle of red wine. She's singing something about being so tired. He tells me it's Jane's Addiction. I don't recognize it. He says she's singing a little out of tune. I ask him if she's okay. He says yeah, yeah, she'll be back or she'll just walk over there to the house on the corner. He points to somewhere near but there's four houses on the corner and which one she's aiming for escapes me. Escapes her. He takes a drag on his cigarette and watches her, smiling. He's probably watched her walk down the middle of the road a hundred times, drinking red wine right out of the bottle singing some Jane's Addiction song. He asks me how long I've known her. I tell him forever, it seems. She was always a little crazy, I tell him. You know, in school she always made everybody laugh. But it was funny because in other ways when you didn't know her, she was so shy, really quiet and he laughs and says, yeah, I don't believe it. And he hands me a beer.

I ask him how long he's known her and he says forever, it seems, and looks at me and smiles. He's got sunken cheeks as hollow as a dead man—a newly-dead man. But his smile makes his face come alive and I'm not much into guys with long hair but his is so spirally and curly, it's adorable and I can understand why she hangs out with him and the other six I've yet to meet. She's told me so much about them. How they saved her life when she was walking off the plank. It's like they just appeared at the right time and took her away from all the bullshit.

A gold Chevy van as long as a horse trailer pulls up in front of us and they flow out of its doors onto the yard. She stops in the middle of the road and turns around. The tallest one calls out to her. She lights up like a ballpark when the lights are flicked on at dusk and she strolls into his arms.

By the time all the beer disappears, she's dancing and laughing in the front yard barefoot. They're listening to something called Temple of the Dog. They're sitting watching her and smiling, taking puffs on their cigarettes, contemplating something. I can't believe she's still standing let alone spinning in circles with no shoes on, singing at the top of her lungs in what seems to be a very quiet, respectable neighbourhood. No one cares here about anything and I just want to crawl under the porch and burrow my way back home. And I'm wondering if I should try and make her come with me. I'm wondering how I can tear her away from the long-haired rock and rollers she's keeping crazy company with and take her back to safety. Reintroduce her to the respectable boy who had a crush on her in high school. The one that did and she didn't know.

I'm trying to think how she'd be if she'd stayed in our town and got married like the rest of us. If she didn't leave for the big city, we'd probably be as close as we used to be. I'm slightly envious of her freedom and long hair, the tattoo on her right ankle and her radiance. Then there's the boys. The guitar players and drummers and singers that look like they're straight off the pages of *Rolling Stone*, and I think I should recognize them; but I don't listen to the radio since I've had children, just in case they pick up on something I don't want them to hear.

Suddenly it dawns on me, I could never have her over to my house. What would she do? What if she brought the band? What if she sang Jane's Addiction songs at the dinner table or danced barefoot in the living room? What would the children think? What if my husband fell in love with her? What would the neighbours think?

She walks up to me and drapes her drunken arm around my shoulder. She makes me look into the sky and asks me if I remember when we used to sit in her backyard and stare at the sky, this very same sky and say one day we will fly. She stares upwards. I tell her I remember. She nods her head and says good.

Pull Gently, Tear Here

She runs the local five-and-dime, sells bubble gum to Boy Scouts and nuts and bolts to handymen, birthday candles and sprinkles to mums. She wakes up at the same time everyday— seven. Doesn't have to work till ten but always, always wakes up at seven. It's a habit. She's been doing that since public school. Her mother, all alight at five a.m. would wake her at seven, get her fed, dress her and send her to school for nine. Two hours of eating, primping, watching the morning television. Stories of hamsters and mice that live by a river and talk, drive boats and wear funny little aprons and top hats. She always swore the river was fake. The fact that little creatures were running around in people's clothes and talking was normal. That was okay but the river was fake.

She went begrudgingly to school. By ten she was tired. Came home for lunch and watched more television. Talking sunflowers and flowerpot men with names like lumberjacks. The mother straightening the daughter's eyebrows and brushing her hair. The mother wiping the daughter's face while pushing her out the door. Just kept on walking out the door with her mother's hands all over her making sure nothing was out of place. Then she gets to school and she's out of place and wonders what her mother's fuss is all about.

She still wakes at seven. Sun barely risen, birds a little sleepy. She wakes and makes tea, sits at the kitchen table and talks to the plants on the windowsill. They talk back and have names like lumberjacks. She waters them just to watch them smile. It makes her feel useful. Then she dresses with her back to the window in her room that has a bed, a dresser and nothing on the walls.

The only light dangles on one wire from the centre of the ceiling and one of the light bulbs—it holds two—is burnt out. She straightens her eyebrows, brushes her hair and leaves.

She leaves early, too early and walks down by the river, along the river and sits on the bench closest to its edge. She feeds the hamsters and mice and they talk about what they did last night and she has a chuckle at their news. Then she checks her watch because now she's cutting it close. She has to open the shop by 9:45 or she just can't get organized. She says goodbye and throws the remaining bread crumbs into the river and watches them float downstream. The squirrels come around after she leaves and eat the bread crumbs in the grass. The ones the hamsters and the mice don't eat.

The Boy Scouts come in at lunchtime, say hello and whisper and chuckle when she turns her back. She thinks she hears something but these little boys are never bad. They'd never chuckle behind her back. Boy Scouts are all good and that's why she likes having them there. Sometimes she gives them a couple extra pieces of licorice and tells them she's ordered new sports cards. They tell her the gum's always stale in the baseball card pack. She says she'll look into that. They take their little paper bags full of sugar, salute her and go back to school. She says, bye boys, be good, I'll see you after school. She dusts and arranges things. Hums and smiles.

Once the kids are in school the mums come out. It's always some kid's birthday and she's got party hat bins, sparkler bins, pin-the-tale-on-the-donkey bins. She's got baby pinatas, ones you can break with a breath but mums still buy them. And some mums bring her shortbread, or some home-cooked thing. Some of them gossip about her odd ways, how she feeds imaginary critters by the river, how she litters the park with bread crumbs intended for furry things in people's clothes that don't exist—and what a shame it is that she just doesn't have a clue. That she just doesn't get it. These mums who smile at her and inquire about her day, tell her she looks lovely and how their kids look forward to seeing her each day. These mums who sit alone when all the other mums go home and stare at their empty living rooms wondering where their husbands are. These mums who watch her walk by when the five-and-dime closes, straightening her eyebrows and hair, taking the flowers she buys on the way to her own mum, who can't protect her anymore now she's passed away.

She wakes at seven, goes into the kitchen, makes tea. She talks to plants on the windowsill, and waters them just to watch them smile. Then she feels useful. She goes into her room, dresses with her back to the window, straightens her eyebrows and brushes her hair. Leaves too early. Walks by the river, sits by its edge, feeds the hamsters and mice, asks what they did last night. Checks her watch and heads for work. Sees the handymen standing with their heads down outside the five-and-dime. At least a couple of Boy Scouts dangling by the scruff of the neck off each one's arms. She cocks her head and keeps on walking towards the shop. She wonders why all the traffic is stopped. She keeps on walking past the sympathetic stares of the mums on the sidewalk. Looking at her and down, and back at her.

She keeps on walking through the crowd, humming, feeling her palms getting sweaty. She can almost feel her mother's hands on her, brushing lint off her navy blue coat, primping her hair, wiping her face. She walks past the Boy Scouts, past the angry handymen, past the smashed windows, crunches over the broken glass, through the already broken down front door, adjusts the floor mat, goes behind the counter and says can I help you?

Havana Radio

The boys throw stones at the passing cars but no car in its right mind would stop in this neighbourhood after dark. So they revel in their mild taste of power. He lifts the cigarette to his best friend's lips. He takes it and says thanks. Then he gets up and walks across the road, down the alley into the blackness. Out of sight and out of their minds. He goes to the only place he knows called home and sleeps while it's quiet. While the other boys slink around like cats in the night and come home richer from the people they have robbed and weary from their travels.

He puts the new batteries in his radio, the ones he stole from the five-and-dime about a week ago. Never got around to changing them, wasn't interested in hearing any music. Sometimes he goes through these phases. Doesn't want to see his pals, listen to his radio, cause trouble or turn tricks. Some days he just likes to walk by the river, past the old ladies, doesn't rob them, sometimes even smiles at them. Past pretty women, handsome men, dogs. Just likes to walk peacefully, non-threatening. Won't even take a second look at the fancy cars parked on the road. Doesn't care if they're unlocked. Has no interest in breaking in. Those days he walks past the hardware store. Sees the young girl, gazes in.

Wants to tell her he can change. That he can make her happy, that after a shower and a haircut, a new pair of shoes, he can be quite handsome. Wants to set up candles on a warm night, listen to some sweet Cuban ballad from his grandma's old radio and dance them into a new life.

All Trapeze Artists and Clowns

My blood rushes through me in waves. At night when the lights are almost out and my closed eyes are wide awake, I can think of nothing but the surge of emotion keeping me up. I can't tell if this is real or illusion. My head is a circus, all trapeze artists and clowns performing tricks, while I'm trying to keep steady, keep still, normal. Sleeplessness is inevitable. 'Cause all the things I need disappear when the circus comes to town.

And I'm wondering if I'm the fat lady, the man/woman, the tightrope walker. Probably the tightrope walker but I can't walk a fine line. Can't even draw a straight line with a ruler. But I'm not afraid of heights. Maybe the lion tamer. The bearded woman. The human skeleton. The dwarf.

Out there on the road, it's all humility and little pay. The only place you could get a job, some would say. We're all freaks, in one way or another. I knew a woman who swung from the high trapeze. No safety net. So beautiful, so tiny. Swung to her death under the big top. Said in her will, she wanted her ashes spread across the Mississippi delta. She had nothing to leave but her costumes and her tiny little ballet slippers. Feet barely bigger than a child's. She rarely used them anyway. She was always swinging around in the air. Had an affair with a clown. The king clown. The one with the rosiest nose, the biggest spitting flower, the reddest, flattest, longest shoes. His own car.

In the circus they didn't like the performers getting involved with each other. Thought it was bad for business, unless you came married of course or they hired you as a team. But who else was there to fall in love with out on the road, travelling from town to town. Performing every night, every weekend, sometimes twice a day. There wasn't any opportunity to date, no time to marry, two days, three days and you're gone.

She came to the circus as a teenager. Ran away to find her brothers. The flying trapeze brothers. Twins. That was always an added bonus in the circus. Twins, tall and handsome. Turns out they both impregnated the same woman at different times on the same day. Almost got kicked out of the circus but the woman gave birth to a two-headed boy. So they stayed. The twins were given a raise.

She showed up in the pouring rain. Thin and weary. She'd travelled by bus and by foot and by train. Kept on searching the papers for the whereabouts of the circus. Had one of those stepfathers who was too loud and mean. She kept on threatening to run away to the circus and he swore he'd track her down, bring her back and ground her for life. She got away anyway. Her mother, timid like a door mouse and just as small, would look at her, like she could stay or go. Her other brother disappeared years ago. No one knows where.

She arrived some Sunday afternoon. Bought a ticket and went in. Bought popcorn and watched the show. Knew then and there she would be happy in the circus. Watched her brothers with pride. Tears falling from her weary eyes. Laughed at the clowns, oohed and aahed at the elephants, and tigers. Shivered when the little man bent himself in half and ate fire.

Laughed again at more clowns. Children screaming and applauding next to her. All wide eyes, open mouths and clapping hands. She sat in the stands till no one was left. Young boys sweeping popcorn bags and candy wrappers from between her feet. She waited there, hoping her brothers would sense her presence and come and find her. Nothing. Silence. Stillness. Then the sun went down. She didn't move. Couldn't move. She jumped when a voice asked her for her name from somewhere behind her.

She turned to see a robust man with a big smile.

"Come here often," he teased. He laughed and lit a cigarette. "Probably a fine little thing like you doesn't smoke," he said. She held out her hand.

"Been smoking since I could," she said and he gave her one.

"Didn't want to go home?" he asked.

She explained she just spent the last two weeks running from there, came here to find her brothers. She's found them, but was too afraid to approach them. What if they make her go back, don't want her around, don't let her join the circus. She started thinking that maybe it's not so easy to just run away and join the circus. What if they're not hiring? No openings for forlorn runaway teens who can't eat fire, bend themselves in half; can't grow beards, swing from thin bars or walk a fine line.

He laughed and told her he ran away twenty years ago. Got himself a red nose and flat shoes and has been running around under the big top, turning somersaults, falling down, getting pies in the face, chased by tigers, run over by little pedal cars and travelling from town to town ever since. He makes children laugh and cry for a meal at the end of the day, and somewhere to sleep. Never thought he'd still be a clown at this age. She says, her stepfather is and they laughed.

He led her out of the big top and around the back to the caravans and trailers.

He stops at a red caravan—all decorative and rickety. He knocks hard three times. A light goes on. A voice yells out, what the hell do you want? She hides behind the man. He says, you got a visitor. Tell it to go away, the voice yells back. She feels her heart sink low like she should never have attempted this. They left a long time ago for a reason and maybe she was one of the reasons. And now that reason has caught up with them and they will not be pleased. Then she thinks that will show them, to think you can just up and leave your family behind. Blood is thicker than water, than distance, than ignorance.

He peeks his head out of the window. She peeks at his face through half open eyes. The man stands aside. Look, he says. The brother squints, rubs his eyes. Squints again. Closes the window and steps outside. He stands real close to her, like he thinks he recognizes something about this girl but can't quite figure out what. She says, "hello". He opens his arms and she gratefully falls into them.

The twins pampered her, fed her, watched over her while she slept. Laughed with her and of course cried. Gave her little jobs to do so she felt useful. She washed their clothes, made meals on the portable stove. She told them she wanted to be a trapeze artist too. She wanted to fly through the air under the big top to the oohs and aahs of the crowd. She wanted to defy gravity, and more.

The twins weren't sure about this. They took long walks discussing the possibilities, the dangers, the benefits. She would wait alone in the caravan with fingers and toes crossed, praying this time they'd come back and say yes, and it didn't happen for what seemed like a long time. She'd given up hope and began to accept the fact she'd run away to join the circus and ended up washing clothes for a living. She didn't mind that much but there wasn't much of a thrill attached to it.

She made friends with the dwarves, the bendable man and the clown. The clown was special. He was more than twice her age but he had an adolescent charm twinkling out of his aging eyes. The twins couldn't know 'cause they would have killed him if they knew he'd kissed her, touched her. They were her good daddies. In some ways. The kind of daddy she longed for but never knew. And now she was discovering that a good daddy's just way too restricting and she had two good daddies to contend with.

She'd meet the clown at night, do his laundry. Massage his weary feet. Hang up his nose and lay away his boat length shoes. Tuck him in and things, and sneak back to the caravan. Usually it worked. And the nights it didn't she'd tell a good lie like any sweet, innocent girl would.

The first time they took her up onto the trapeze she felt a stirring in her stomach. She felt like she could do anything in the world. They lowered the bar so that when she fell the net was only a few feet below. The big drops would come later. She swung and fell and swung and fell till her back, hands and neck ached. She'd drop and get back up and drop and get back up.

The twins were decidedly proud with her progress, and they figured a young pretty girl in a leotard with long flowing black hair and ivory features could only be good for the show.

The clown, always hovering somewhere in the wings, unsure of her safety, wished she was content washing clothes and making dinners. She might outshine him one day, had all the makings of a main attraction and that just may not do.

She would sneak off in the night less frequently. By the end of the day she ached and was exhausted, couldn't use the clothes washing excuse anymore. If the twins were out, some nights, he'd sneak over and comfort her as best as any clown could do. And she'd fall asleep in his arms, whispering things to him like thank you and I'm sorry I can't rub your feet tonight.

The first time she was ready to perform, she picked up a little pink outfit from the fat lady who, before she became the fat lady, had been a very slim, beautiful trapeze artist. The fat lady gave her a few pointers, well wishes and the thumbs up, then handed over her little pink leotard and ballet slippers with sequins and rhinestones coating the front. She was very moved and told the fat lady she'd do them proud.

She swung to the oohs and aahs of the crowd and felt more exhilarated than any clown could ever exhilarate her. She was flawless and each time she performed she asked the twins to raise the bar higher and higher. She swung alone more often and became a main attraction. The clown hovered in the wings, frowning beneath his painted on smile. Saw her less and less.

She signed autographs after the shows. Little girls dressed up like her. She got paid more than the fire-eater, even more than the lion tamer.

The clown left her dried flowers on the foot of the caravan steps, along with his red nose and stick-on-tears. He just disappeared that day. Probably ran away to another circus. That's the thing about the circus, there's always another one to run away to. She was sad. She did love him. He did treat her like no man had treated her, except the twins, but that was different. She changed a little that day, started taking bigger risks and acted like nothing really mattered but swinging up there in the air. Turning somersaults in between flying off one bar before grasping onto the other. She never missed. Never faltered. It was the one place she was flawless, untouchable.

She had the safety net removed. The twins were outraged.

They argued with her till they were all in tears. She refused to listen. She wanted to prove that she was the best. She wanted to become the biggest attraction. They begged her, pleaded with her but the net was not brought back.

She climbed to the top of the ladder with a conviction she'd not experienced before. Flashing through her mind was the day she left home, the bus rides, the walking, the cold, the hunger. She pictured the clown, how she did love him at one time.

She pictured her mother—if she could see her now, the man married to her mother, if he could be beneath her now, her father and she reached the top.

She grabbed the bar, a chorus of oohs and aahs reverberating against the big top. She looked down—you're never supposed to look down. The twins' eyes peering into hers. She closed her eyes and moved into the air, hands clutching the steel like they'd never clutched anything before. She felt the wind against her face, the noise of the crowd a muffled din. She remembered the first night on the steps of the caravan, her brother's face peeking out of the window, their arms embracing her. Their words, their love, all they did for her and all she wanted was for them to forgive her when she released her grip that day.

I'm Thinking

Always wondered if one day I might just run away and join the circus. Didn't have to, it joined me.